A Dream of Wolves

WARRIORS OF THE OLD GODS

RHIANNON FUTCH

Contents

One

Chad told me to stay at the house once I arrive. He knows. He knows that woman didn't go up in flames all by herself. Knows that his sister is a murderer. I didn't have to set her on fire. There had to have been another way to stop her. I should have done more, found another way. I should have been studying more with my magic. Her death is all my fault. She didn't have to die.

Matthew steers the car into my driveway, puts it in park. We sit here for a moment in silence. He starts to speak and I think I can't take it if he tells me he hates me or that he can't look at me again. "You don't have to stay. I understand if you need to go. I'll be fine here at the house." Opening the car door, I get out and slam it as I run for the house.

He is right behind me when I open the door, anyway. Following me in the house, he pushes the door closed and pulls me into his arms. He feels nice, comforting. My arms slip round his waist as my head leans on his shoulder. He says, "I'm not going anywhere. You are where I belong. And you are not okay right now. There is not a chance in hell that I will leave you alone with your thoughts. Come, let's get you seated. We need to research your grandmother and find out who that woman was. Maybe it will help distract you."

I let him lead me to the couch, staying there while he grabs my laptop from the bedroom. Every time I close my eyes all I can see is her face as she burned. The way her flesh seemed to melt and drip off her bones. Matthew sets the laptop in front of me on the coffee table and I type in the password. He quickly realizes I am not going to take the lead on researching my grandmother and turns the laptop to face him as his fingers fly over the keyboard while he sits on the floor in front of the coffee table.

There is a knock at the door, and I get up to answer it. Chad is standing there, still in uniform. He takes one look at me and his arms come up, pulling me into a bear hug. "Where is Matthew? Why isn't he comforting you? What happened out there?"

I can't really talk with my face pressed into his chest and I realize my face was wet when he smooshed me into this hug. I must have been crying and didn't realize it. I bring up my hands and push against his chest. He releases me but puts his hands on my shoulders as if he is worried I'll fall down without the extra support. "Why are you crying?"

"I'm crying because I'm a murderer. Because all I see when I close my eyes is her face as she burned. Are you going to arrest me? You probably should."

Chad sighs and pulls me over beside him as he moves further into the house and shuts the door behind him. "No, I am not here to arrest you. In fact, I am fairly certain we have your case pretty well closed. But why is Matthew sitting there on your computer instead of concerning himself with your well-being?"

Matthew meets my eyes at that and looks surprised. "Because I didn't know she was crying? She wasn't when I started researching." He stands, "Blaze, can I get you some tea? Or anything? Do you want to sit here with me while I research your grandmother? Would you like for me to just hold you and put off the research for now?"

"No, I'll be fine. I'm just coming to terms with being a murderer."

Chad gives my shoulders a squeeze. "Sit down and tell me what actually happened. Then we'll decide whether or not you are a murderer."

I sit on the couch and Matthew talks as he paces, telling him about recognizing the woman as one of the women that kidnapped him. How she had incapacitated him with her magic.

Picking up where he left off, I tell my part. "I was hiding beside the car when she came around it. She brought her hands up to shoot at me and I threw mine up just to block whatever she was going to do. I wasn't expecting… the fire. It just shot out of my hands, like it had a life of its own. I didn't know how to stop it. When I did get my hands to close, there wasn't much left of her. I killed her because I couldn't stop the fire. She didn't have to die. There had to be another way to stop her."

Chad comes to sit next to me on the couch. He grabs

me by the shoulders and turns me to face him. "Listen, that lady fully intended to kill you. She is well known. The file we have on her is thick. She kills people for money. The only reason we haven't had her in a prison is because she always uses magic. Always. So we can't pin it on her in the human world, even though we know it was her. Hell, half the time she sticks around the scene just to watch us clean up after her."

"What? Really?"

"Really. She was hunting you. She definitely would have killed the both of you. What you did was self defense. Now, what I want to know is, why was she hunting you?"

"Um, it probably definitely has something to do with the preacher that is after me. I don't know why, but it looks like he hired my grandmother to have Matthew kidnapped. They might be a little upset about the rescue."

Chad frowns. "What rescue and why didn't you call me?"

"I didn't call you because you wouldn't have let me go in first to distract them while Falina and Frankie went and found Matthew."

"You're fuckin' right, I wouldn't have! What do you mean, you went in first to distract them?"

"I mean exactly what I said. It was me they wanted. So I went in and bought them time to get Matthew out. Besides, it's not like I can't defend myself. Fuck, I just murdered a woman earlier tonight."

"That wasn't murder and you still should have called me."

"I had to do it. They had Matthew in a cage in the

basement of the church. Everything didn't go exactly the way we planned, but everyone in our group got out safely."

His expression changes to surprise as he says, "Wait, the church fire was you?"

I look away, ashamed of the death and destruction that follows me like some cursed cloud. "It was."

"Holy shit Blaze. Why is he after you?"

"I'm not really sure? It started out as James trying to get me back, but why would they all get in on it this hard? It doesn't make sense for the Pastor to be after me this way just so James can have the girlfriend of his choice."

Chad nods and says, "It doesn't make any sense. You're my sister and that makes you special to me, but it seems weird that other people would go to these lengths. There must be something more that we are missing."

Matthew

My phone rings at the worst possible time. Looking at it, I see it's Fen. Well, I call him Fen. Should I explain to them that his name is Fenrir, and he is the Fenrir? That Odin is still not friendly with him and he is definitely not friendly with Odin? Maybe I should just let them figure it out. It isn't my story to tell. Walking away so I don't disturb their talk, I answer. "Are you here yet?"

"Your pants are in a fine twist, aren't they? I'm just getting to town. You didn't send me the address."

"I'll send my location now."

Fen ends the call without even saying goodbye. I hope Blaze won't hate him. I need to work closely with him, and I can't do that if she refuses to have anything to do with him. Seating myself in front of her laptop, I work on researching her grandmother some more while Chad talks with Blaze. I am finding shockingly little about the old witch. There's another knock at the door and Chad tells Blaze he will get it. She nods, and he walks to the door. He opens it to find Frankie facing the other way. I hear him ask her, "Who was that?"

Frankie says, "No idea. Some rude asshole. Want me to bring him back so you can check?"

My stomach drops. It had to be Fen. Chad says, "Yes, bring him back."

She focuses a little and what I assume must be Fen comes tumbling back to the yard in front of the house. I race to the door as Fen stands up. "He's actually with us. I'll bring him in with me after we talk." Frankie giggles as she walks into the house behind Chad, who leaves the door standing open. Nosy. "Fen, you just got here. How did you piss her off so fast?"

Fen shrugs, "It's a fucking talent. What can I say? Do we need to be here with the angry witch or can we go have a drink?"

"I found *her* Fen, and she is in danger. Unfortunately, the danger she's in is tied up with our mission. My Gertrude, I can't leave her. I need you to find a way to get along with these witches, at least. Can you do that?"

He rolls his eyes, "Please tell me her name isn't Gertrude this time."

"No, her name is Blaze. Can you tone it down? Apologize if need be?"

"Yeah. I know she's the reason you got tangled in this whole mess. I'll behave for your love and her witch friends."

Two

Frankie walks straight over to me and hugs me hard as she sits down on the couch by me. She asks, "What happened? Why are you crying?"

All the stress comes pouring out and I cry into her shoulder. She rubs my back, murmuring, "It's all right. You just let it all out. We'll get you sorted."

It takes a minute to get myself under control. Frankie is super patient and doesn't rush me at all. When the sobs calm down enough that I think I can cope with the rest of the world again, she senses it and releases me. Chad hands me some paper towels and I wipe away mascara, tears, and clean up my nose that decided to run after I sat up. I hear Matthew talking to someone outside and I turn to look as they walk in the house. Matthew walks in and I am comforted by his presence. Then he moves to the side and lightning hits me as I lock eyes with the stranger.

Oh gods, what is wrong with me? The wolf side of me is frantic to get to this man, and I don't want to stop her.

I'm the evil they keep saying I am. How could I not be when I love Matthew so much and all I want to do is plaster myself to this stranger? I feel like I've known him forever, but I've never met him. I vaguely hear Matthew introducing him to everyone. I think I said something in response. I hope I said something coherent in response. Fucking hell, I have to get out of this room. I can't think with him so close. I look to Frankie and point at the kitchen;, she nods and tells everyone we are going to go make some tea and talk in the kitchen.

After nearly running into the kitchen, I grab the kettle and fill it with water. Frankie said tea and tea is a great idea. Maybe I can forget how evil I am if I drink the right kind of tea? Shaking my head at my own foolishness, I put the kettle on the stove and turn on the burner. I am still staring at the kettle when Frankie asks, "Are you ready to tell me what is going on?"

"I killed a woman tonight. Chad says it was self defense, but I set her on fire, Frankie. I watched her burn to death. It doesn't feel like self defense when I watched her burn. It wasn't fast and there was melting. Then I staged the scene, so it looked like she was burned with the car. I really think I might be the evil that the pastor thinks I am."

"Nope. You are absolutely not the evil he thinks you are. For one, he is an idiot. He doesn't know what he is talking about. For two, you couldn't. It just isn't in you kill without reason. Do I believe you could intentionally kill someone and maybe be glad about it? Yes. But that doesn't make you evil. Honey, evil is that there are still people that would have us burnt for existing if they knew exactly what we are. That is evil. You killing someone in self-defense, not evil. Even if you were relieved or happy that she died."

She seats herself at the table and waits as I put the tea together, a cup for each of us. I set hers in front of her as I sit in one of the chairs next to her at my little table. Looking at her, I tell her, "There is one other thing, but I can't say it where all the sharp ears out there could hear me."

Frankie nods and holds up a finger. Then she closes her eyes and makes some motions with her hands as she whispers some words that I don't quite catch. When she opens her eyes, she says, "They won't hear you now. Unless they walk into the room. Say what you need to say."

"That man that walked in with Matthew, I feel like I know him. Like every fiber of my being, including the wolf side of me, wants to reunite with him so badly it hurts. But I've never met him! I'm either crazy or evil. Probably crazy evil."

Frankie chuckles, "Considering the guy, whose name is Fenrir, you might be a little crazy. But what if you did know him in a past life? I mean, you knew Matthew. You felt a connection with him, and still do, right?" I nod yes, and she continues. "Well, what if you knew this guy, loved him too, in another life that Matthew wasn't a part of? Maybe your past lives are coming back to haunt you in some weird way. I think we should talk to Glenda about this?"

"Yes, that is a brilliant idea. She is older, been around long enough to have seen some things. Maybe I can hold off on deciding that I am evil until I talk to her. Maybe this is a thing with witches? Immortal lovers find them again in other lives, sometimes at the same time? Oh my god, I can't have two boyfriends."

Frankie shrugs, "Why not?"

My jaw drops. Recovering a little, I ask, "What?"

She sips her tea and says, "Why not have two? I mean, as long as everyone is on board with it, there is no reason you shouldn't. Honestly, if you can find two men that don't make you want to murder them, I say keep them both."

"You think that's possible?"

"Polyamory is a whole thing. Give it some research. You are not the only person who has ever loved more than one person."

"How do you know all this? Are you?"

"No, not really. I sort of dated a guy that was for a little while. He was a decent guy. I just never got that into him and we eventually drifted apart. We are still friends. I could probably ask him for some solid sources for you, make your research a little easier."

"That would be amazing. Please do. I need to know that this isn't as evil as I've been led to believe it is. I don't need extra reasons on top of the murder."

Three

∝

BLAZE

A knock sounds at the door. This place is so busy tonight. Frankie drops the spell that kept the guys from hearing us. One of them answers the door and then my father is rushing into the kitchen, his eyes looking a little wild till he sees me sitting and drinking tea. The aunts follow behind him, looking much more calm as my father hugs me and asks if I'm ok.

"I'm ok. I wasn't hurt. Really. I was the one that did the most hurting of other people."

My dad watches my face as I talk. I don't know what he sees, but he nods and says, "I'm going to tell you a story. I haven't told this to anyone. So you'll all hear it for the first time." He walks over to the counter and leans against it as my aunts take the other two chairs at the table. Watching the floor like it might move, he takes a deep breath and says, "After your mother dropped Chad off, she left us alone. I am fairly certain that she couldn't bear to be near us and not part of our lives. Your grandmother, she was never so good. For a solid year after Chad was born, she sent witches to kill me. She wanted to end our existence because it was a stain on her family name."

"Oh no, Dad, how did you manage?"

His face hardens. "I killed them. I killed every single one of the witches that came after us. Murdered them one at a time for daring to come after my family. I spent a year murdering at least one witch a month. I don't know if your grandmother ran out of witches that would come after me at that point or if she just gave up. Every one of those murders was self-defense and defense of my family. She wouldn't have stopped at us, she would have gone after the rest of the family with us out of the way. I couldn't risk that."

Ell is scowling as she says, "Why didn't you tell us? We would have helped you."

He shrugs, "I didn't want them to come after you too."

I can't help but nod in understanding. I would have done the same. Ell doesn't miss my nod, scowling at me as well.

My dad says, "I killed twenty-seven witches before she stopped sending them. They were all so young. I hated doing it. Hated taking their lives from them. Hated myself for doing it. But there was no other way."

Ell nods, "He is right. I wish he would have let us bear some of the burden with him, but I understand why he kept it to himself." She slants a look at him, saying, "If you ever hide anything like that again I'll beat you within an inch of your life."

He laughs and says, "I promise I won't tackle repeated murder on my own again."

That woman would have killed Matthew and me, given the chance. I'm not for sure that I'm not some sort of evil, but maybe killing her isn't why.

Leann clears her throat. "We all are very glad that you had the strength to do what had to be done for the safety of you and yours. I, and everyone here, hopes that you will always be strong enough to do what must be done."

"But what if she wasn't going to kill us? Maybe she was just going to bring us to Grandmother."

Matthew and Fen appear in the doorway. I am struck again, seeing Fen and Matthew side by side, wanting them both. Then Fen says, "She would have killed you both. Witches can be evil too."

Four

MATTHEW

Fen looks distracted, but I can't focus on that right now. Right now I need to ensure that he doesn't try to kill Frankie for turning him into a tumbleweed. "I know you are probably still upset about what Frankie did." The voices in the kitchen are loud enough I can hear them out here. I want to go to her, but she needs her family more than me right now and I think the best thing I can do is work at making sure Fen behaves. "But she is Blaze and my friend. I need you to let it go. Can you do that?"

Fen is still looking toward the kitchen. He hasn't said a word or even acted like he heard what I said. I tell him about the things that have happened, including the witch that just tried to kill us and that Blaze's grandmother probably sent her. He nods, but mostly seems focused on the conversation in the kitchen. Then Blaze says, "But what if she wasn't going to kill us? Maybe she was just going to bring us to Grandmother."

Fen growls and heads for the kitchen, me right behind

him. Fen stops just inside the doorway of the kitchen to say, "She would have killed you both. Witches can be evil too." He takes a breath and continues, "When I was a young creature, there was a witch that had a deep grudge against my father. So deep that she told my grandfather a prophecy that destroyed my life. She didn't care who suffered so long as my grandfather lived in fear. Her prophecy has reverberated through the ages and destroyed any hope we ever had of being a family. She was a seer. Why would she lie? My grandfather believed every word she ever said, even after finding out how she was always seeking revenge on my father. You must believe me when I say some witches are nothing but evil. Just the same as everyone else. I can promise you that if a witch knocked Matthew out and was stalking you, she was planning for both of you to die. Do not waste your heart on guilt over an evil one."

Fen

Matthew goes to her as she struggles with the idea that she needed to kill the witch. I watch as he kneels next to her chair and puts his arms around her. My vision is all red. I want nothing more than to tear him apart. How dare he touch her? She is my mate! But no, she is his mate, his Gertrude come back to fuck with us all since she is my Glenna too.

I can smell the way she recognizes me. Smell the wolf in her desperate to get to me. See it in her eyes when she looks at me. Fuck! I can still see the way she looked last time I saw her, her blood soaking the ground and my clothes. It was ten years before I killed every member of the gang that murdered her. And I could have killed them for another ten year had I not run out of gang members.

Blinking to clear the images from my mind, I realize her aunts are eyeing me hard. My fists are clenched and I am probably scowling pretty hard. Shit. As I work to unclench my hands, I hear Matthew suggesting that we go get food for everyone. Perfect. "That's a great idea. Ladies, we'll return with food. Gentlemen, you can have some too."

Matthew laughs with everyone else, completely oblivious to how much I want to rip him to shreds for being the one she smiled at. The one that got to touch her, be touched by her. Leaving the kitchen, I get myself outside and take some deep lungfuls of air that aren't scented with her. With Blaze. What a perfect name for her. The gods are truly fickle and I fucking hate them. I wonder if this is Odin's doing? Did he do this to fuck with me? Test my control to see if he could get rid of me finally?

If he did, I'll make that fucking prophecy come true. Maybe this is what the witch saw. Me, confronted with the woman I love more than anyone in existence and knowing that I can't have her because she is also his Gertrude and fucking Matthew found her first. Dammit.

Matthew comes out, "Hey Fen, are you okay?"

"Yeah, I'm fine. I just needed some air. That's a lot more people than I've been around in a long time."

"Oh, damn. I'm sorry. I didn't even think about that. You never stopped avoiding people after her, did you?"

"Unless I was there to kill them, no." Oh god, Matthew. If you had any idea how close you are to being one of those people. "Let's go get the food. I'll follow you. I need the wind."

The wind rushes through me, pushing away everything. Everything but the smell of her blood on my hands as she died.

Five

BLAZE

I watch as Matthew heads out to join Fen and I could cry with relief, if I weren't already crying about being a murderer. I see my aunts watching me. Their thoughts are damn near written across their faces and I can't tell them they're wrong, so I look down at the table.

Falina arrives and Frankie answers the door, I can hear them as Frankie catches Falina up on what has happened. I could hug them both for being so staunch in their claims that I was defending myself. But no one else defends themselves till a woman is burnt crispy. Anyone else would have given her the opportunity to run away.

My aunts get up, and Ell says, "We need tea. Erik, Chad, find more chairs. The kitchen is the right place for things like this, but we'll need more chairs. Go."

I watch as they get up and leave the room, seeking chairs that don't exist in my house. I hear the front door open and close and I know they immediately realized that, too.

Falina comes in and hugs me. "Oh honey, even if you melted the bitch, it's not murder. Grams would say the same. Will say it if I call her. Should I call her and let her tell you how silly that idea is?"

"Are you all sure? I really feel like burning someone crispy turns it into murder. I should have found a way to let her run away."

Leann laughs and says, "No. Making sure they are really dead doesn't make it murder, even if it seems a little extreme in hindsight. Never let someone that is trying to kill you have the chance to run away. That just gives them a second chance to kill you."

I feel something in me loosen. Maybe they're right. All of them say it isn't murder. Maybe I need to let it go. Which will probably get easier when I don't see her burning every time I close my eyes. Ell puts another mug of tea in front of me, picking up the other one she says, "Drink. You can't change the past and the future is always yours to choose. However that looks."

Fuck me. I nod and start sipping the tea. That woman can see straight to the heart of me and she knows. She knows I love Matthew and that Fen is a pull like nothing I have ever felt before. Was that approval of whatever I decide? I need to talk to her and Leann sometime, alone. Until then, I will just smash these feelings down. My wolf feels unhappy about that plan, but I can't do anything else right now. I have too much to deal with just in trying to survive. Chad and our dad come back in bearing chairs. Falina, Frankie, and I cast a spell to expand the little round table that works great for small groups, not so much for this crowd.

About the time we get the table and chairs situated, Matthew and Fen come back with a huge spread from the Italian place down the road. The smell of the food fills the small space, giving me a reprieve from smelling Fen. We eat and try to discuss the preacher and his desire to possess me, but Aunt Ell and Aunt Leann keep guiding the conversation away from that until we all are having a good time, laughing and carrying on.

As long as I don't look at him. Fen, why am I so drawn to you?

Fen

Matthew leads me to an Italian place down the road. It's packed, but the food smells good. It smells strong, which is even better. We get in the door and ask for a to-go order;, the hostess tells us it will be a wait to get it but they can accommodate us. Matthew tells her, "That's fine. We can wait. Do we put in the order with you or will one of the waitstaff come to take our order?"

"One of the waitstaff will get it. If you could have a seat in the chairs just there?" She points to a set of chairs off to the side of the entry. We thank her and move over there, letting other diners be seated or given a little buzzer.

We sit in silence for a minute before my curiosity, no, my need to know about her, gets the better of me. "Tell me, what's Blaze like now that she is Blaze and not Gertrude?"

Matthew gets this smile on his face and I hate it so

much because it is on him instead of me. He has had time to get to know her this time. Because he is part of her life. He says, "She is a lot more confident and protective of those she calls family. At the same time, she is more fragile. I think what hurts her will define the reaction. Hurt her family and the hurt goes poorly for someone else. Hurt her and she might go into seclusion for the rest of her life."

"Ah, and that is why she feels so bad about the woman that died earlier?"

"I think so. I think she intended to throw her hands up and block, not go on the offensive, so to speak. She is so strong, Fen. When I found her, she was with this piece of trash that she doesn't want dead yet because she wants him to live with the shame. This guy was hitting her. He put her in the hospital. When she broke up with him he went to the preacher, pastor, I get all their fucking titles confused these days. He went to him to force her to get back with him."

Sounds like he needs to have an accident. And I am just the wolf to arrange it. "What was his name?"

Matthew eyes me and says, "Oh no. If you kill him, I'll be blamed. We are going a different route. She was working for a mortuary that is a big supporter of that church. Now she works at mine and I am expanding to put him out of business. I am buying the company her ex works at and I am going to have them go through everything he has ever done to verify its legality. I will bring him down with his own actions. I've already had pictures of him hitting Blaze posted at his office. Worry not, my friend, he will suffer. His end will not be quick nor merciful."

The server comes over and takes our order;, she tells us it will be a half hour to forty-five minutes before it is ready. Matthew tells her that's fine and she hurries off to put in the order.

"So, she is a shifter this time, but her grandmother is a witch?"

Matthew shrugs. "Yes, but she isn't just a shifter. Technically, she is mixed. Her mother is descended from a long line of witches. A long line of powerful witches. Her father, well, he was the older shifter man back at the house. The younger one is her brother. Erik and Chad, she found them by accident, oddly enough. From what I understand, her mother got pregnant with Chad young and her parents threw a fit. So she abandoned Chad with his father. Years later, she's married to this stuffed shirt kind of guy and trying to have a child with him, but can't get pregnant. She figures out why and goes to see Blaze's father. A happy little weekend. Who knows how she convinced him to do this, but then she goes back home and a month later tells the husband, it worked. She has Blaze, and Blaze's power comes in, but it's fire. The grandmother inspects little Blaze and binds every single piece of magic in her, along with her wolf. Stripping her of the time she would normally have been learning how to work with her power and her wolf."

"What? How is Blaze okay after that?"

"Well, I get the impression that she wasn't for a long time. Honestly, her control over her power isn't great yet. It's better, but she hasn't had access to it for very long. The only time it was able to come out before was when she was in danger and it didn't always come to her aid then. Most of the time, she was trying to hold it back so she wouldn't hurt anyone. She didn't even know about her wolf side till she found her brother."

"What the hell is wrong with her family? Who would do that to anyone?"

"Well, her grandmother seems pretty fucking awful based on what little I have heard. If I understand correctly, she rules the family with an iron fist. The mother has been directly under her thumb all her life, to the point that she didn't even argue with her about the binding of her daughter. If she even knew it was happening until after."

"That is insane. Who is the grandmother?"

"Her name is Pamela Smythe. She is the leader of a coven of really nasty witches. Including the one that Blaze ended tonight. She is, from what we have found so far, at the least, working with Pastor Ward. Possiblly more. We don't know much in that area yet."

"How did you two meet?"

"I was in a cafe to meet with Odin and do some work. He left and a few minutes later, she walked in. The minute I saw her, I knew. She was so nervous that day. I told her I was new to the area and looking for a good church. She ended up inviting me to hers. She was so sweet, trying to be the person she thought she had to be. Her ex was shitty to her the first time I showed up at the church. And her trying to reassure the prick. He didn't deserve her. I'm not sure I do, but I'm going to do everything in my power to be deserving of her."

Fucking Odin. Of course, he was involved. "Is she happy now?"

He smiles like he can see her face. "Yeah, I think she is. She smiles so much more now. She got her own place after getting a new job. She has women around her that have her back in ways that I think maybe she has never experienced. She found the other side of her family and they are better to her, care more for her, than her mother's family could ever begin to manage. Every time I do even the smallest of things for her she is delighted. Tonight, the plan was to take her out. It just got a little derailed."

His every word is another shard of glass twisting in my heart. She's happy. My woman is happy. I can't take that from her. She's got this whole network of people that I sure as fuck couldn't replace if she gave them up to be with me. And Matthew is my friend. One of the precious few people I would term friend. I can't take her away from the good that she has found, no matter how much I want to crush her to me. Twisting the glass a little harder in my heart, I say, "That is really great. I'm so glad you two found each other."

He goes on, telling me how happy he is and I hate the whole fucking world and every god in it for setting this up. The server walks over to us, pushing a cart with four large bags. I stand and offer my card before Matthew can pay for it, the server takes it and walks away, saying she'll be right back. As we wait for her, Matthew tells me stories of their outings. I hate hearing them and I'm hanging on every word about her. The server brings my card back and I sign, making sure to tip her generously. Stuffing the card and receipt in my pocket, I grab two bags off the cart while Matthew grabs the other two. We make it out the door, being very careful to not jostle the bags too much. After we get them all loaded into his car, I tell him, "I'll see you there."

I spend the ride back to her house cursing Odin.

Six

BLAZE

Walking through this field, beautiful as it is, I can't help but wonder how I got here. I'm surrounded by a sea of forget-me-nots. I don't know if they even grow around here. Peacock feathers rain out of nowhere as a voice whispers, "Remember…"

Suddenly, I am watching myself in a bar. I don't look like me now, but I know this woman I am watching was, is, me. An arm slips around me, and suddenly I am looking out of her eyes. Looking up at Fen smiling down at me, saying, "Let's get out of here." I feel safe with him, like nothing in this world could possibly touch me. My wolf is purring with the pleasure of his touch. We leave the bar and get on his motorcycle. I snuggle up to his back, my arms clasped around his waist. A short ride later and we are at a house. Getting off the bike, we are walking toward the house wrapped up in each other when I bolt upright in my bed, heart pounding and my body throbbing with need.

My alarm sounds and I groan. Looking at the clock as I

shut it off, I realize this isn't my first alarm. This is the get-up-now-you-are-going-to-be-late alarm. Fuck! Running through the house, I start coffee and then shower as fast as I can. Even as I race through getting ready for work, the dream won't leave me. Most dreams fade with sunlight and the start of my day, but this one? The one that could cause the most problems? It sticks like glue. Even as I rush around like a mad woman getting ready.

I make it to work, just barely clocking in on time. Falina takes one look at me and asks, "You and Matthew have too much fun last night?"

"No, he went home because I just wasn't feeling great and besides, he has Fen in town. Do I look that bad?"

She laughs, "No, you look great, actually. But I figured you must have been playing sexy games to end up wearing a peacock feather to work."

My heart beats frantically as adrenaline shoots through my body. I reach up to find one perfect peacock's feather tangled in the hair that I washed and brushed before I left the house. Staring at the feather, I know my dream was no dream. Though I wish it was just a dream. Everything would be some much easier if I could believe this was just a crush, not another lover from a previous life. And Hera making sure I remember. Was she the one that sent me all the dreams before?

Falina taps me on the shoulder. "Hello! Earth to Blaze, where did you go? We need to get this guest prepped for cremation."

"Yes, sorry. Let's go."

We begin prepping the woman, and I can smell the magic on her. I know this magic. This is my grandmother's doing. And the way she died… it's horrific. I stop and look up at Falina. She looks as upset as I feel. "You feel it too, don't you?"

"I do."

"Is there anything we can do to fix this?"

Falina shrugs. "She's dead. Her soul isn't here. The best we can do is a spell to release her and cremate her and release all the ties that she has attached."

An idea hits me. "Falina, do you think we could skip using the fuel and let me do the burning? Let me cremate their remains with my fire instead? Use it to give her a sort of blessing as part of her send off, since it was my grandmother that did this?"

Falina looks around to make sure no one else is nearby. "Do you think you can control the burn?"

"I do. I've been practicing a lot and I think, I think maybe using it this way might help me feel less upset about, well, last night. And about what my grandmother did to this poor witch."

"All right. We can definitely shut off certain tracking bits while still tracking temperature and progress. Can you sustain it for that long? I mean, looking at this woman, I'd say it will be at least a two-hour burn. maybe two and a half."

"I do. I know I can do this."

"All right. Let's check on where everyone is and what they are doing. We don't need anyone wandering in while you cremate a guest. Even if she is one of us."

Everyone else is busy and will be for the next several hours, with the funeral going on the other side of the building. The preparations take very little time. The spell is fast and doesn't require more than us and some symbols drawn in the air over her body. Once we get our guest in the crematorium, Falina operates the control panel and gets it set up. With the display showing all that we'll need to monitor, she gives me the go ahead. I call my powers and light a fire inside the crematorium. It is quickly up to the temperature. Holding it steady at that temp is not the easiest thing, but I manage it.

Two hours later, I have been holding the temp within a degree, more or less of the desired temp, and Falina checks the guest. The guest is now ashes and bone fragments, ready to be collected and placed in the memorial urn waiting for it. I extinguish the fire and we let the crematorium cool as Falina congratulates me on maintaining such rigorous control for so long. She tells me, "I've never seen anyone hold power like that for so long. This is really rare, to be able to do that. I wouldn't tell people about it too much. Even witches get jealous."

I am tired but so happy that I was able to do this with no problems. Maybe I can fully claim my magic and do some better things with it. "No, I wouldn't dream of telling anyone about this. I'm just happy I managed to do this, to seal her away from my grandmother."

Falina hugs me. "You did so good. Grams is going to be so proud of you when she hears about this."

"Do we have to tell her? I don't want to worry her with the reason we did this."

"We can omit the part about why and just say you wanted to try it to practice your control. It's close enough to the truth."

Matthew

"This graveyard smells weird."

Fen shrugs, "They aren't the first ones to bury new ones over the old. People should be glad they haven't gone back to tossing them all in a pit. I know I am. That smelled so much worse."

"Yeah, they did. Did any of the gods give you a protection from the pastor?"

Fen grunts, "Yeah, Freya did. Odin still worries about being in a room alone with me. She didn't mention why. Is this one special or something?"

"He seems to be picking up powers and getting real close to being one of them. If he manages that…"

"The world crashes out because we don't just have a lunatic leader, we have another deity with a lot less sense and a ready power source in his current cult. Fuck."

"Exactly. Between that and his interest in Blaze, we need to get rid of this guy without anyone realizing it was not an accident or a natural cause."

"Why is he so interested in Blaze, anyway? I mean, didn't they get the memo that you and Blaze are together now? I know they ignored the one about her not being interested."

"I don't know if they know Blaze and I are dating."

"Dating? Not together?"

"Yes, just dating for now. She just got out of a bad relationship and isn't ready for more than dating right now." What the fuck is Fen up to with this line of questions? Why is he smiling now?

"So you two aren't exclusive right now. That's great news."

The pastor chooses that moment to leave the building. I turn and head for the car, telling Fen, "Maybe we could keep our minds on the following the pastor instead of *my* Blaze?"

Fen is grinning ear to ear as he says, "But she isn't exactly your Blaze now, is she? We can let the topic go for now, but I won't forget."

I don't like the way he said that. I don't like it at all.

Seven

FEN

The pastor has been inside his mistress's house for hours. It looks like he plans to spend the night there. We've been holding up a tree down the street for just as many hours. I think we could just come back in the morning and find him still here, but Matthew has wanted to stay so far.

He is getting real antsy now, checking the time every minute or so. I wonder where is he supposed to be? My belly is feeling really damn empty, so I suggest going to get some food as I start walking toward the car. I have no intention of going hungry for this shit. He can stay if he wants. I have other ways to travel.

Matthew sighs, falling in step beside me. He says, "I'm supposed to be meeting Blaze and Chad for dinner shortly. I was hoping this fucker would be back home by now. They can't still be fucking. Right? He is still mostly human."

"I don't know if you know this, but men and women

do more than just fuck. But why not invite Blaze and Chad to join us? Unless, of course, you're scared. I mean, I would understand if you are worried that having her around me might make her forget about you."

Matthew glares at me as he calls Blaze. "Hi, how was your day?" He pauses as she tells him about how she cremated someone with her fire and how she held the temp for two solid hours. Matthew looks as proud of her as I feel. "Blaze, that is amazing. All your hard work is paying off. I'm so proud of you."

I refrain from telling her how proud I am of her. I know it would just be weird since we technically just met. I listen as she says that she is going home to change out of her dead people clothes and asks where she should meet him and Chad. Matthew slants a look at me before he tells her, "Things ran late with Fen tonight. Do you mind if he has dinner with us?"

Blaze says, "Oh, um, yes. I mean, I don't mind if he comes. What I mean is, yes, he can have dinner with us. The more the merrier, right?"

I would swear she got flustered just now. And had some Freudian slips if my dirty mind is picking up what she is saying correctly. Gauging by the grumpy look on Matthew's face, I'd say I have read her right. Matthew ends the call pretty quickly after that, saying, "Fantastic, we'll meet you at your place and you can ride with me."

He looks at me and says, "Best behavior motherfucker, best behavior."

I just smile at him, "I'm always on my best behavior."

Of course, there is the possibility that our definition of best behavior may differ a bit.

Matthew

I don't like it. Fen is entirely too interested in my Blaze. My Blaze, dammit. I can't lose her. She's everything to me. I know she feels the connection between us, though she fights it.

I really don't understand what the fuck is going on here. Fen has never behaved this way around any woman. He's only dated the one that I know of and he kept her far away from all of this until it found her, anyway. Last I knew, he was still avoiding people in general. Why is he suddenly so interested in the one woman I have been waiting on for nearly a millennia? It doesn't make any sense.

This should be no problem. Fen is real damn rough around the edges and the center for that matter. He'll offend her saying something rude and I won't have anything to worry about as long as I continue to treat her like the queen she is. This is going to be fine. I have nothing to worry about. Blaze may be fighting our connection, but I know she loves me. She would do just about anything to avoid hurting the ones she loves.

Why does this Fen thing feel like it is going to be a problem? Blaze texts me she'll meet me at the restaurant. As I get in the car, I text back, "Sure, no problem. I'll see you there."

Now I need to get there before Fen.

Eight

BLAZE

Fucking hell. Fen is coming to dinner. I have to find some way to keep myself together, I cannot let anyone see how he affects me. Sending Matthew a message, I tell him that I will meet him at the restaurant. I need the space to get myself together. It takes very little time to put myself together now that Falina gave me the spell to get the smell of death and formaldehyde off me. I am especially happy that it gets the smell out of my nose as I start the drive over to the restaurant.

Plus, I really don't want to smell like death around people with such sensitive noses. My wolf perks up as the thought of sensitive noses brings out little flashes of memories. Memories with Matthew and Fen. Seperately, but still, am I crazy? Why am I the one all these things are happening to? I don't think any of this is even remotely normal and I sure as shit do not understand why I would have all these memories. This isn't how it's supposed to be, right? I always thought, you die and go on to the next life with no memory of the previous one. I shouldn't have these memories, dammit.

Pulling into a parking spot, I look around to see if anyone else is here yet as I put the car in park and shut off the engine. Chad is two spots away, getting out of his car. Excellent. Grabbing my purse, I get out and head towards him. He greets me with a hug and then looks at me critically, asking, "Are you all right? You look stressed."

Great. I guess between the witch that I uno reversed when she tried to kill me, the women that have been coming in mutilated by our grandmother, and the complications with Matthew and Fen, I probably look a stressed mess. "It's nothing. I've been having weird dreams this week and not sleeping great."

Chad frowns. "What kind of bad dreams? Are they prophetic?"

"No, no, nothing like that. Just run of the mill bad dreams. Really." He narrows his eyes and looks like he wants to press further. So I say, "Let's go get a table while we wait for Matthew and Fenrir to arrive."

He frowns, but nods. As we walk toward the door, he says, "You'd tell me if it was something serious, right? Like an attempt on your life or something. You wouldn't hide it from me or forget to tell me?"

The relief that he is willing to let this go is damn near a physical reaction. I push the door open as I say, "I definitely would tell you if it was something important like that. This is just bad dreams and stuff. Honestly, I would have called you the last time something like that happened. I just lost track of time. Plus, still adjusting to the whole people care about my welfare thing. It's a little weird."

"I don't understand that last part, but I don't need to, so long as you know you are cared about now. I'm here for anything else too, but I'll let you keep it to yourself if you aren't ready to talk about it right now."

The hostess gets us seated quickly at a table for four, and Chad sits across from me so we can easily continue chatting while we wait for Matthew and Chad to arrive.

I feel it when they walk in, the very air in the place feels charged with their presence. I look toward the door and they are walking our way, Matthew not even slowing for the hostess as he says, "We are with them."

Fen is grinning as he sits in one of the chairs. With Chad across from me, the other two chairs are on either side of me and I am realizing I didn't think about the seating arrangement nearly enough as Fen looks at me, "How's your day been, beautiful?"

Chad raises a brow at me as Matthew leans over to give me a kiss with a pointed look at Fen. As he seats himself, Matthew asks, "How has your day been, my love?"

"Uh, my day has been that I managed to hold my power at a steady flow for a little over two hours today. So I'm thrilled about that accomplishment."

Chad says, "Congratulations! That is awesome, we should celebrate."

Fen waves at a server. They nod to acknowledge him and our server shows up shortly after. Fen asks for a bottle of wine for us all, then turns to me, "What is your favorite kind?"

I feel my face heat, "Um, I like reislings."

He turns back to our server, "We'll take a bottle of reisling and four glasses, please."

The server asks, "Would you like an appetizer with that?"

Matthew answers, "We would love the sampler of appetizers, thank you."

The server nods and leaves to tend to our order. Chad is fully entertained at this point, and I can't even blame him. The server brings the reisling and the glasses, telling us the appetizer platter will be out soon. Fen pops out the cork that was mostly opened and pours in all four glasses, handing me one before finishing the pour. The other two glasses are handed over and Matthew says, "A toast to Blaze, all the hard work she has put in is paying off and I know she is going to soar."

We all drink and the server comes back with the platter. Matthew and Fen each pick up a plate and place little bits on them and present the plates to me at the same time. I accept the plates, thanking them both, though I am beginning to feel like I can't breathe.

Standing, I say, "Chad, walk me to the bathroom please."

He chuckles as he stands. "Excuse me, gentlemen. We are going to the bathroom."

I can feel their eyes on me as we walk toward the bathroom. Happily, it is across the restaurant and around a corner. As we turn the corner Chad says, "Is this what has you losing sleep?"

I nod, and he laughs. "Well, now I get it. Sorry for laughing, but it is kind of funny from over here."

Groaning, I say, "Could you please just keep this to

yourself? I really don't need to be hearing it from anyone, especially not the aunts. I plan to talk to them, but I really want to tell them myself, beyond what they have guessed."

"No worries, but considering that they each have multiple boyfriends I think maybe they would be more understanding than most. But I'll do you one better. If the aunts do find out from someone, I'll be just as surprised as if I never knew."

I nod, "That suits me just fine. I'll be out shortly."

He nods and leans against the wall as I push into the bathroom. It is cool and quiet and blissfully empty as I take care of business. Washing my hands, I get them rinsed and after shaking them to get most of the water off; I press them against my face. It calms me and I take a deep breath to further the calm feeling. I don't know what to do here; I feel pulled to both of them. I know Matthew and I are just dating, but I don't know how to handle this. A guy pursuing me I could deal with. But the way I want Fen, oh gods. I must be some kind of evil to be this torn about it. Especially since I want Matthew just as much.

Matthew

Watching her and Chad walk to the bathrooms I tell Fen, "You're making her uncomfortable."

He chuckles. "What makes her uncomfortable is how much she likes it. I smell nerves and excitement, not discomfort. And I know you smell the same thing. The one thing she was uncomfortable about was being celebrated. Why is that? Who did that to her?"

Sighing, I say, "That was her parents. Her father was never pleased with her being his only heir and having the audacity to be a girl. Her mother was never able to be out from under the grandmother's thumb. I mean, what her grandmother did was unforgivable, but the mother not only allowed it, she told Blaze that it was necessary. They never wanted her unbound. They planned for her wolf to die and leave her half a person." Taking a deep breath, I glance toward the bathrooms, making sure they aren't on their way back. "Look, I know you are going to be trying to charm her. I'm resigned to that and I trust her. I don't fucking understand why you would suddenly be after my Gertrude. For tonight, though, let's just tone it down. She has a lot going on and I think she's had about all she can take since she ran away to the bathroom."

Fen looks toward the bathrooms and back at me, nodding. "I'll trust your judgement since I don't know this her as well as you do, yet. And the reason, I don't think you are ready for that. The gods are assholes."

Don't know this her as well as I do? What does he mean by that? And not ready for what? Opening my mouth to ask, I see Blaze coming back to the table. Damn. I'll ask him later.

Nine

FEN

Matthew's house is nice, but he favors delicate shit that I feel like I'm going to break if I bump into it. Today, I am hanging out at the bar. Not much that will break here and this one has the bonus of being close to her work. It's the closest I can be without being a creep hanging outside her job. This feels like the only kind of home I've known since she died. And now she's back. I know she wants me. I just don't know what is holding her back. I mean to find out, though. It might just be she worries about how Matthew is going to feel about it. If that's the case, I can just continue to flirt in front of him. Eventually she'll—holy shit. That can't be her. But it sure as fuck is my Blaze walking into the bar and ordering a double rum and pineapple. A man that wants to die follows her, stepping up next to her and saying, "What the hell do you think you're doing in a bar?"

She turns, a look of surprise and then aggravation on

her face when she sees him. She snarls at him, "James, I am in no mood for you. Go away."

Ah, so this is the ex. Good. I stand as he says, "You have no business being in a bar. And you haven't returned any of my calls or messages. It is unspeakably classless of you. My importance has grown now that Pastor Ward has designated me as one of his apostles. You'll need to do better as my wife."

She slams her hand on the bar. "Listen," the bartender delivers her drink, and she turns to thank them and then back to James. "What I do is none of your fucking business. I'm good with being classless and I will never be your anything ever again. Now go away Judas, I'm in no mood."

She turns away from him and picks up her drink. She is just taking a sip when James grabs her arm, causing her drink to spill down her shirt. He says, "You aren't—"

Anything else he wanted to say is cut off by my hand around his throat. As I lift him, the bartender says, "The dumpster is out back."

"Excellent. Blaze, you stay right there till I get back."

She grunts as she blots the spill off her shirt. I lower James enough that he can sort of walk on his toes if he stretches and focuses on the ground instead of struggling. When I find the dumpster out back, I stop long enough to tell him, "She is under my protection. I catch you following her again and I'll make you disappear."

He shouts about how I can't throw him in the dumpster, but I grab the back of his pants with my other hand and toss him in like day old garbage. He lands with a wet sound and I think maybe this isn't the bar's dumpster.

Oh well. I walk away as he is retching and hollering about how I dare.

Back inside, I find Blaze standing exactly where I left her, halfway through her drink. Stepping up behind her I ask, "What's got you day drinking?"

She jumps and spills her drink again, "Jesus Fucking Christ Fen! My shirt was nearly dry. Honestly, you know I am in here day drinking and it must be for a reason. Why would you not walk up next to me like a normal person?"

"Ah, there she is. There's my little feral wolf. Come sit with me, before one of these idiots makes a move on you and I have to kill them."

She looks around and sees the men that are eyeing her. "Fuck. Okay. Wait, you didn't kill James, right?"

"No. I didn't. Matthew told me you didn't want him dead. If I catch him bothering you again, I will."

She turns around and looks up, scowls at me, and shoves me back. I let her because she is fucking adorable when she is surprised like that. I point at my table and she leads the way. Gods, I could watch that forever.

We sit and I ask again, "What has you day drinking?"

She looks away. "I just have a lot going on." Then she looks me in the eye and says, "Which you aren't helping with."

I can't help but smirk as I tell her, "I'm not here to help you stay with anyone else. I came to help Matthew with a particularly troublesome pastor. Imagine my surprise at finding my favorite feral wolf back in the world."

Her eyes go round. "What do you mean, back in the world? And how do you know about the wolf?"

I lean in to say, "Darlin', I can smell the wolf in you.

What I don't understand is why you smell like woman and wolf, not wolf woman."

She shrugs. "That is an easy answer. We haven't been one for very long, we are still integrating. My grandmother did terrible things that have only been recently undone." She downs the rest of her drink before continuing, "And apparently, she is working with the good pastor. She thinks I am an abomination."

Nodding, I say, "She's allowed to be wrong."

Blaze laughs and then frowns. "Why are you making my life so complicated?"

I gaze into her eyes, "Because I couldn't do anything else from the minute I saw you."

She sets down her glass. "I have to go."

I stand with her and follow her out the door, easily keeping pace with her as she strides across the lot toward the little diner.

She looks at me and asks, "Why are you following me?"

"Because I'm keeping you safe."

She chuckles, "I think I'm safe enough in the awful waffle."

Chuckling, I tell her, "Perhaps, but I'm going to make sure you get home safe, anyway."

She says, "I hope you like greasy eggs and steak."

I tell her, "I've had my fair share of it, don't worry. I'll be fine."

We get inside and talk while we order and devour our food. She is smart and funny and I would stay here forever if it meant I could listen to her. Her feral nature keeps peeking out and I want to help it out into the light. She is magnificent when she gets that little violent gleam in her eyes. Eventually our meals are finished, and she asks for the check. I snag it and go to the counter to pay.

My little feral wolf thinks she is going to sneak out while I pay. She's so cute. The server hands me my card and the receipt; I scrawl my signature and write in a tip before I dash out the door and catch up to her as she reaches her car.

"Where are you going?"

She leans back against the car. "I'm going home Fen. Where I should have been hours ago."

"Great, I'll follow you and make sure you get home safely."

She tells me, "You don't need to. I'm a big girl and can get myself home just fine."

"I know you are, but I don't care. I'm going to do it anyway, so I know you got home safe."

Blaze shakes her head and says, "Suit yourself."

Putting my hands on the car to either side of her, I lean in close to her and whisper in her ear, "Blaze, if I suit myself, I'll be coming... inside."

Her breath catches and she says, "I'm leaving now Fen."

My grin is wide as I push away from the car and trot over to my bike. She's definitely not immune to me.

Ten

BLAZE

Every sense in my body fires up alarms as I pull into my driveway. Fen stops behind my car and says, "Blaze, come here. You forgot your purse in my saddlebag."

The wolf in me is whining even as I was trying to sense the problem, but I back toward Fen slowly, never taking my eyes off the house. When I get within reach of him he grabs my arm and tugs me close to him, telling me in a low voice, "There're witches here and they don't smell anything like friendly."

I pull my phone out of my pocket like I just got a message and I send out SOS texts to Falina and Glenda. My phone pings like mad with messages saying they are coming. Luckily, they have my location all the time anyway, so they know where I am.

Fen is telling me, "You need to leave with me now. Let me get you out of here."

Matthew pulls up and gets out of his car looking unhappy as he focuses on Fen's hand on my arm and the way he is leaned in talking quietly to me. But then he slows and looks around, feeling the weirdness in the air. He is nearly to us when something comes flying at me from the house. Fen snatches me back and we land on the ground, me on top of him on his back. Matthew dove toward the cover of being behind my car even as I twisted around to fire back at the spot where the shot came from. My fireball hits a wall of illusion and it shatters, falling to the ground like glass to reveal five witches standing on my damn porch. Matthew grabs Fen's legs and pulls us behind the car.

Another car screeches to a halt behind us and then Falina and her family are pouring out of the car as I roll off Fen and come to a crouching position.

Glenda gets us all in position and then she says, "On my mark, we fire. We are going to teach Pamela that she doesn't get to mess with one of ours."

I want to cry with the feelings this unleashes in me, but there's no time for that as she says, "Now!"

We stand and fire as a group. There are seven of us. Not every shot hits, but at least two of them do. One witch falls to the floor of the porch, unmoving. Another one falls with an injury but keeps firing at us as her fellow witches leave her behind.

We keep firing at the witches that are running away as Glenda shields the injured one. She gets to her feet and staggers a little out into the yard, but she is bleeding pretty heavily and doesn't make it far before she collapses.

Eleven

FEN

We stood ready for any physical attacks, but the witches turned and ran when they realized they were out numbered. Two of the witches were hit. One is definitely dead. The other lives, for now. I look at Matthew. "Stay with her?"

He nods his agreement and I jog across the yard to the witch laying in the grass while keeping watch for the ones that ran away. I am immune to most magics, but that doesn't mean they can't hurt me, just that it doesn't stick. I crouch next to the woman and ask, "Who sent you to kill her?"

The woman laughs. It turns into a bloody cough. When she recovers, she says, "Her grandmother."

"Why?"

The woman turns her head to glare at me, "She is a filthy abomination who never should have been born."

Falina growls from behind me, "Move away from the trash."

I stand and back away from her. I am no more than two steps away when the woman sinks into the earth and it closes over her like she was never there. I look at Falina and she shrugs. "She tried to kill my friend and then decided to be extra shitty with the reasons why. My tolerance for those idealogies is all gone. Besides, she was almost dead anyway, and I got to make sure her last moments sucked more. Sometimes we get to be the karma. The western version of it, anyway."

Shrugging, I tell her, "I approve. Not that you need the approval. Agree is the better word. I agree with you."

She nods, "It's fine wolfman. Go follow Blaze around."

Grinning at her, I get to them in time to hear Matthew ask why I am here. Before she can answer, I say, "I found her at the awful waffle, so I stayed with her while she ate and followed her home, just in case."

Blaze agrees, "Yes, that." She looks relieved, but Matthew doesn't notice as he is watching me when she says, "He was being a pest and it worked out."

Matthew says, "Thanks, Fen."

Blaze says, "Yes, thank you Fenrir."

I smile at her. "You can call me Fen."

Blaze

Well, I guess since Fen is what I've been calling him in my head all this time, it's good that I have permission before I fuck up and call him that out loud. Matthew is frowning and studying the two of us. I know he can probably hear how fast my heart is beating with the two of them focused on me. I just hope he can't smell the rum from earlier. Thank fuck Fen didn't mention it and covered for me. Not my finest moment, hiding the drinking, but I need something to burn away the image of the women that keep coming in mutilated and bound to my grandmother.

And I'm certainly not ready to tell anyone about what my grandmother is doing. I don't even want to think about it myself. Falina is keeping it quiet too, because she wants to talk about it just as much as I do.

Falina takes a step to be right next to me and I wonder how long she was behind me listening? Falina says, "We cleared the house. Those witches weren't taking any chances. They couldn't get in the house, but they were able to squish the shield inwards. They also set some very nasty spells that would have set the house on fire when you walked in. Grams is pissed."

Just then, Glenda calls my name. "Blaze, could you come here, please?"

Excusing myself, I hurry over to where she stands on my porch. "What can I do for you?"

Glenda says, "I recast the spells they had on the house without the dangerous parts. I want you to learn how to search for them."

It doesn't take me long to spot the signs. Once I have spotted them all, she teaches me how to eliminate the spells without triggering them. Once I've done it three times over, she says, "Why are you connected to these men?"

I freeze. "What do you mean, connected?"

She says, "It's like there are strings connecting you to both of them. They are thicker with them so close, but there is another one stretching off into the distance that is spider web fine."

"Is that bad? It sounds like it might be bad."

Glenda studies Matthew and Fen, saying, "No. They look like they are old though. As if these connections happened in other lives. I only say other lives because you aren't old enough in this one for the aura of age these give off."

Turning to watch them, I think about what Matthew said about I was his wife once upon a time. "What the hell the gods were thinking when they did this? That I should live in torment for the rest of my life?"

Glenda shrugs. "Maybe ask Hera about it. The way the sparks fly between the three of you, I would be surprised if you weren't meant to have a relationship outside of the norm. Some other time, ask me about my husbands."

My eyes round as my jaw drops, "Husbands? I had been meaning to ask you about this anyway, but you had husbands? As in, concurrently or consecutively?"

She grins, "Husbands concurrently. More than one at a time. Witches are a little less restrictive about these things. Mostly." She tugs me over to the circle of witches. We all clasp hands and perform a spell to keep the fog of forgetting over the neighborhood. I am mostly trying to just follow along, as it's my first time doing this spell. It only applies to strange things, paranormal things, but it will help to keep us safe from people that might decide we need to bring back the dark ages.

Twelve

MATTHEW

Waking up in her bed is a fantastic way to start my day. Especially after yesterday. Fen is wasting no time trying to get close to her. When she allowed me to stay, it was all I could do not to cheer. Sitting up, I see light peeking around the room darkening curtains. Probably still fairly early, though.

I look down at her and find tears running down her face as she sleeps. I wipe away a tear, asking in a whisper, "Love, what's making you cry?"

She answers, still sleeping, "He was so sad when I died. It's breaking my heart."

I ask who and she says, "Fen. He's crying over my body. He looks as sad as you did."

My heart freezes in my chest. What the fuck? How? It can't be. Easing out of bed and grabbing my clothes on the way out the door, I close it gently behind me. In the living area, I dress and then move into the kitchen. It's farther from the bedroom and maybe I won't wake her up. I pace the small kitchen, my head spinning with the implications. Coffee. I'll make coffee. As I make the coffee, I try to think about which deity I will get the most direct answers from. As I fill the carafe, I see a peacock's feather in the window. I'll call Hera. She is usually pretty direct with her answers, and she is obviously trying to connect with Blaze. "Hera, I have some questions and I would like to speak with you." She appears immediately, a sly smile on her face. That smile says it all. I snarl at her. "You know why I've called you."

She nods. "But you'll have to ask the right questions."

What? Frowning, I ask, "Why? Why do I have to ask the right questions?"

She says, "Even gods can be bound to not offer information." She seats herself at the table to watch me. I fill the coffeemaker and push the button to start it.

Pacing again, I think hard. I know I have a limited amount of time before Blaze wakes up and I need to make these questions count. I stop and face Hera to ask, "Has Blaze has lived more lives than the one with me and the current one?"

She smiles, "Yes. Good question."

I think for a moment before I ask, "Was she hidden from me in those lives?"

"Bad question."

I growl in frustration. Ok, that was a bad question. Is it because she can't tell me that or because it is irrelevant? "Were her other lives with Fen?" She waits for me to clarify, and I say, "All?"

She says, "No."

"Any?"

"Yes."

"More than one?"

"No."

I pace for a bit. Then an idea hits me and I stop to ask, "What is the purpose of this?"

She grins. "Ah, that is a very good question. The purpose is control. Think Lord of the Rings, the one ring."

Her patience while I sort this in my head is appreciated. Horrific understanding dawns on me. I look at Hera and say, "One woman to control us all? They set us up to all love her? Set her up to love us?"

Her smile fades as she nods.

Looking away, I ask, "Why?"

She tells him, "They need you to win this war against Pastor Ward. Now ask me how I am involved."

I ask and she tells me, "I tweaked things. I am what is causing her to remember the loves from her past lives as she meets them. The other gods planned on her being a pawn, turning to them because she thought she was evil. They were going to make her think they were making a special allowance for her because she was needed. They had no intention of letting her know they planned this from the beginning. They intended that she be a pawn to further their ends rather than allow her to take part or not of her own free will."

And that is when Blaze speaks up, "They were going to use me to control them by making me think I am evil?"

I turn to see her in the doorway, hair still a mess, soft pajama shorts that barely cover, and a pajama tank at capacity. My heart squeezes in my chest painfully at the look on her face. She looks at me. "Are you going to leave me?"

Blaze

Matthew looks stricken by my question, but I have to know. I hold my breath as I wait for him to answer. He crosses the room and takes me in his arms. "No. Not for anything. Whatever happens, you are where I will be. Am I super happy with the idea of sharing? No. But I would rather share you with whoever you are connected to than lose you. You are why I chose to stay, to work with the gods. Much like Fen in your dreams, killing everyone involved in your murder didn't bring you back. I would drain this world dry to be with you."

His words break me a little and I cry. He holds me and tells me it will be all right over and over until my tears dry and I straighten up. He moves his hands to my shoulders. "Are you feeling a little better now?"

Taking a breath, I nod. "I think so. Is that coffee I smell?"

He says, "It is. Go sit and I'll bring you a cup."

Sitting down opposite Hera, I say, "I still don't know if I can get involved with anyone else. It seems like I would just be playing right into their hands."

Hera smiles, "It is. But you have no choice. You will need them all, and you are the only way to unify them."

"Great, so I have no choice in the matter? None at all?"

She lifts a shoulder and drops it. "You have a choice,

but all choices have consequences. If it can't be done one way, you'll have to find another way to stop what is coming."

"What exactly is coming?"

She sighs. "I can't tell you much. But I can tell you the other gods are focused on the wrong threat. The real threat isn't from the pastor. Is he a threat? Yes. But he is nothing compared to your grandmother. And you are the only threat to her."

"What? Why me?"

Hera laughs, "You would call it an accident of birth. But the machinations of the others and myself made you the best possible adversary for her. Not that everyone was aware that was the goal. Her own actions made certain that you wouldn't have an attachment to her, and she accidentally served our purposes in that way. We intended for you to be strong enough to lead them into battle and not die. If you die, we would lose the others."

"Well, that is super. I would say I'm glad she could work so well for you, but I really wish she hadn't."

Matthew sets a cup of coffee on the table in front of me and pulls a chair closer. He sits as I pick up the cup and take a sip. The warmth spreads through my chest and things seem a little less dramatic. "I was tweaked to ensure I am what exactly to my grandmother?"

Hera smiles, "Hopefully, the reason for her downfall. The one person strong enough to bring about her death. Admittedly, they thought it would be Pastor Ward you needed to fight. You will need the help of your lovers, but you are the focus and the one she fears most. That fear will make her reckless. Make sure you aren't. I've stayed too long. Think carefully before you make your decisions."

Hera disappears, leaving me with so many questions and even more doubts. Matthew slides his chair around so he is directly in front of me. "How are you, after all this?"

"Not fucking good, that's for sure."

He chuckles, "That's fair. How much did you hear?"

"Most of it. The walls are thin and you trying to get out of the bed without disturbing me set off my alarm bells. James did that, and it usually meant he was going to snoop around my house and find a reason to yell at me. Or worse."

"Shit. I'm sorry."

"You didn't know. How would you? I'm sorry you had to figure this out by talking to Hera."

"Well, um, actually, you kind of told me."

"I what?"

"You were crying in your sleep and I asked you why. `

"Super."

"Its good things are out in the open. You can decide how you want to proceed, and I will act accordingly."

I sip my coffee to give myself some time to think about this. "I don't know what I want to do. What I should do. What if I fuck it up?"

"Then we'll fuck it up together. Love, you were meant to do these things. Am I thrilled they kept us all in the dark? That they used you in this way? No, not even a little bit. However, I haven't even been able to be truly mad at Fen for trying to get closer to you. I didn't like it, but it was always your choice. If you find that this is what works for you, then that is what we will do. You are so strong, and that strength has always been one of your best qualities. You make your decision and know that I am behind you or wherever you want me, for as long as you want me. Even if you decided you no longer want me, I am still yours and still supporting you."

And now I'm crying into my coffee. Work should be extra fun today.

Thirteen

FEN

Waking up in Matthew's house is strange. I am sleeping on this giant bed and I wonder if I brush against the carvings, will they crumble into a thousand pieces? I haven't seen her in days and I don't have a good reason to seek her out beyond this deep desire to see her again. Fuck it, I'm up. Dragging myself out of bed, I put on a pair of cutoff jeans and wander out for coffee. Matthew is dressed like he has places to go and board meetings to run when I make it to the kitchen. Luckily, he made coffee already. As I am pouring mine, Matthew tells me, "We need to talk."

Raising a brow, I come to sit after my coffee is sorted. "So talk."

Matthew says, "I know she was with you in another life."

The spot between my shoulders tightens and I say, "Oh? And how are you taking that?"

"Yes, oh indeed. She dreamt about her death with you a couple of nights ago while I was there."

I look down into my coffee as if it will erase the memories. "That wasn't a good time."

"Believe me, I understand. From what I heard, our reactions were remarkably similar."

"You murdered everyone too?"

Matthew nods and I raise my coffee cup in a toast, "To killing the bastards before they take her this time."

Matthew raises his cup. "I can drink to that."

Fen says, "Since you know I can't walk away from her, what now?"

"That's the complication. It isn't just us. And we were all set up."

A spark of rage wakes up as I ask, "Odin?"

"He is part of it. It was all of them. Hera is the one I called for information. She meddled and gave Blaze more information, to resist the feeling evil part they planned to use to control her with. She was always meant to be their pawn."

"My little feral wolf is no one's pawn. They didn't think this through."

"They didn't. And they missed a bigger threat while trying to make sure they had us controlled."

"Bigger threat?"

"Yes. Blaze's grandmother. Hera said she would need all of us to combat her. Which means two things. One, we have to take out Pastor Ward as soon as possible. And two, we aren't the only ones."

"I got time today. And plenty of frustration to work out."

Matthew sighs. "You know it isn't that easy. I wouldn't

have called you or the others if it was. He is just a few more worshippers from becoming a god himself."

I laugh, "Gods can be killed too. Ask Odin what he fears most. What does any of this mean for Blaze and us? Are you saying you won't stand in the way?"

"No, I won't stand in the way. But I won't be stepping aside either. She hasn't made any decisions. I am with her, whatever she decides."

"Fair enough. I can agree with that." Eyeing Matthew, I say, "I suppose if I have to share her, there's worse people I could be stuck with."

Matthew snorts, "Shut up fuzzy, and try not to shed in my house so much. It took a month to get out all the fur last time."

Laughing as I stand with my coffee, I head back toward my room, saying, "I told you blowout season is fierce."

Blaze

Thank fuck this bar is close to work. There were three of them today and I just can't take it. Getting out of my car, I hit the button to lock it as I am walking away. The cool darkness inside the bar is refreshing. The light of day felt blinding. I don't even look around, just straight to the bar. I'm probably going to need a ride home, but it's fine. I'll call someone later. I don't want to deal with the questions yet. Not while the images are so freshly burned into my brain. She must've been angry about the severed connections. I made it so much worse for these women.

I order a shot of whiskey and a soda. When Fen comes up behind me and whispers in my ear, I don't even flinch, just down my shot and motion for another. Taking a sip of the soda while the bartender pours, I can feel his eyes on me. Guess I won't have to call for a ride. I down the next shot and Fen says, "Come on. We're going for a ride. When I stop, you're going to tell me what upset you like this." Then he tells the bartender, "Put her drinks on my tab." He gives Fen a thumbs up as he takes my shot glass away. I want to be annoyed, but the shots are kicking in and I am feeling a little fuzzy. Fen pulls out his phone and calls Matthew. I hear Matthew say hello and Fen says, "She's with me. Something upset her and I'm going to take her for a ride".

Matthew says "Call me when you know," and ends the call. What a strange reaction. James would have hit the ceiling and then me. Fen's big hand wraps around my arm and turns me toward the door. I decide I may as well go along. I've never gotten to ride a motorcycle. He takes my purse gently from my hand and stuffs it into a saddlebag. I watch as he gets on the bike. He turns to look at me and I feel a strange sense of déjà vu when he says, "Ride with me, Blaze."

I feel like I'm in a trance as I climb on behind him and clasp my hands around his waist. He makes sure my feet are in the right spots and fires up the bike. Five minutes down the road, the tears start and I'm crying into his back. He puts a hand on top of mine and holds them. I don't know how long we rode, but when the tears stop and he pulls over, it is full night. We are in a clearing with dense woods surrounding it, only the trail we rode to get in open to the outside. After he shuts off the bike, he unclasps my hands and tugs me to one side. I take the hint and stand on shaky legs as I get off the bike. Swiping at my face, I sniffle a bit and try to get myself together. He gets off the bike, plants his feet and folds his arms over his chest. "All right, we're stopped. What upset you?"

I look at him, my heart breaking for those women all over again. "Do you really want to know?" My voice is raw, strange to my ears. "You be real sure about that answer. Because it is fucking horrendous."

He simply says, "Yes."

I pace back and forth as I tell him about the women. How they've been coming in mutilated with arcane symbols carved into their flesh. Choking back a sob, I tell him, "That isn't even the worst part. Women come in mutilated all the time. Maybe not with arcane symbols etched in their flesh, but it is a regular occurrence. No, the worst part is they come in smelling like magic. My grandmother's magic!" I realize I screamed that last part and I clap my hands over my mouth to keep from screaming more. I feel the horror of what she did bubbling up and I curl in on myself to try to keep it from escaping. Next thing I know, Fen has me in his arms and is hugging me tight. I find myself sobbing again. How could she? Is this what my grandmother plans for me? How can I be related to someone so fucking evil? He holds me till I stop crying again. I apologize for ruining his day.

He says "This has been the highlight of my day. Don't worry about it."

I look at him in disbelief. When I recover sufficiently, I say, "Man, what the hell kind of day did you have that this is the highlight?"

He laughs and says, "Fair enough, but I am glad I could be the one to catch you when you are falling. How are you feeling?"

"Like I had two shots on an empty stomach and then cried entirely too much. My head feels a little stuffy, but it's clearing out. Mostly, I'm heartbroken and horrified. I knew my grandmother wasn't a good person, but I never dreamed she could be so evil. And seeing the results so up close. I've been cremating them myself. Falina and I have been casting spells at work to release the women. Then I use my power to cremate them, just to be sure. It's the only thing we could think of that would help these poor women."

"Falina is dealing with this too?"

"Yeah, but she is handling it better because it isn't her Grams doing it. We agreed to keep it between us as long as we could. It's horrific and we don't want to burden anyone when we can't stop it. Why make everyone go through the horror?"

"So you cremated three women today? One at a time?"

"Yes. I had to. I couldn't let them…"

"No, I understand. Let's get you home. You are going to need to rest. Excellent work on the magic. I know it must have been really hard to hold it together and do that while you were falling apart inside. Next time, you just send me a message. I'll come get you and we'll ride. Ok?"

"I don't have your number. And I don't know if I should. I, did Matthew talk to you?"

Fen tensed when I said I didn't know if I should have his number, but he says, "Yes, he did. I know all about it. I take it you are still unsure?"

"Well, I haven't had the opportunity to even ask how you feel about this. I know how Matthew feels. What about you?"

He smiles and hugs me. "I feel like it was a dirty, underhanded move for them to do this to you. The idea that they would think my little feral wolf could be manipulated that way for very long is laughable. I think that even if Hera hadn't interfered, you wouldn't be their puppet for long, if at all. I am mostly aligned with it. Will it take some adjustment? Yes. But I didn't think I would ever see you again and having you here, there isn't much I wouldn't do to keep you."

The relief flows through me, and I sigh with it. "Thank you. I was so worried about what the connections would do if—"

"Wait, what do you mean, connections?"

"Remember the day the witches were waiting at my house? Glenda pointed out that there are cords, so to speak, running from me to you and Matthew. And at least one more that she saw stretched super thin, like a strand from a spider web, stretched off into the distance. Essentially, you are both bound to me. I was worried about what would happen if one or both of you rejected me. I don't know what those cords would do."

His shoulders drop and he says, "I do. Because I've lived it all this time. It feels like a hole inside that nothing can fill. It's always there, always yearning for the one person who could fill that space. It is a continual feeling of emptiness, no matter what you do. No matter the revenge, drugs, alcohol; none of it can even touch it. It is sheer misery even as you try to live and do your job."

My heart breaks for him. How long was he living like that? "How, um, how long was it like that for you?"

"You died around sixty years ago."

"Oh Fen, I'm so sorry."

"I'm sorry I didn't protect you well enough."

"I can't put you both through that. And it's not as if I don't feel the pull toward you both. I just really didn't want to hurt either of you or make anyone miserable."

"My feral wolf, the only way you could do that is to turn us away. You let us figure out how to get along with this. Beyond that, as long as you are happy, we are. Now," he pulls me back with one arm around my shoulders, then leans down to slip the other behind my knees and pick me up. He walks over to the bike and sets me down next to it. "We are taking you home so you can rest. I'll take you to work in the morning and we'll pick up your car after work."

Fourteen

MATTHEW

I've been waiting here for hours. Luckily, her porch is comfortable and the house knows me. Fen sent me a text a little while ago, letting me know they were on their way back and he would catch me up when he got here. The text helped, but now I find myself listening for the sound of a motorcycle.

Finally, I hear it. It's Fen's bike. I'd know that sound anywhere. I watch for the lights of his bike and something in me eases when I see them. I stand as they pull in the driveway, eager to see her. Fen helps her off the bike and pulls her purse out of his saddlebags. She looks shaky and sad, but on the mend. I'm glad he found her and was able to help. She steps onto the porch and looks at me; I open my arms for a hug and she steps into them. Wrapping my arms around her as she does the same to me still feels as amazing as it did so long ago.

She releases me and walks into the house while I stay on the porch with Fen. We listen to the shower start before we speak. I ask him, "So what happened and is there someone we should kill?"

Fen says, "A lot. It's been going on for a little while and she didn't want to talk about it because it's fucking horrific. And we already have orders to go after this one." He continues on, telling me what she told him about the women coming into the morgue, the mutilation, and the scent of her grandmother's magic heavy on all of them.

I look toward the sound of the still running shower as if I could see her in there, saying, "She's been keeping this to herself? No wonder she is so upset. Where did you find her?"

"At a bar not far from her work. It's a dive, but still a good place. It was as close as I could get without a reason, so I've been hanging out there when she is working. She walked in and downed two shots before I got her out of there."

"Well, I am staying here tonight. You?"

Fen says, "I'm not leaving her like this."

"She has one full size bed and a short couch."

"Guess you better get real comfy being close to me because unless she says otherwise, I will be sleeping next to her tonight. And really, I think it will help her feel more secure to have us both there."

"I agree. I guess we should go wait for her to get out of the shower."

Blaze

Getting out of the shower is hard. I could stay there for an hour or three. I'm sure they have both gone home because I am certainly no picnic to be around right now. After drying off, I hang up the towel and open the bathroom door to go find clothing in my closet. As I step out I see the two of them laying on my bed, I shriek a little with the surprise and dart back into the bathroom, slamming the door behind me. I'm still standing there, back against the bathroom door, when Fen says, "Don't put clothes on for us. We're fine with you walking around naked."

Oh, my god. They did see. All of me. "I didn't realize you two were still here."

Matthew chimes in, "We aren't leaving you alone tonight."

Wrapping a towel around myself, I take a deep breath to try and slow my still racing heart. Opening the door, I walk out, and Fen whistles low. My face heats with a massive blush as I walk straight into the closet and shut the door behind me. Grabbing some night clothes, I am very grateful to know my closet well enough to do this in the dark. Yes, my night vision got better once I merged with my wolf, but it isn't that good.

Exiting the closet, I go back to the bathroom and hang my towel up. Turning towards my bed, I see they are both fully clothed, shoes and all. I tell them both, "Get your fucking shoes off my bed."

They both drop their feet to the floor, start taking off shoes. I need to get ok with this one day; I guess today is as good a day as any other. I crawl into the middle of the bed and get under the covers. Now I'm laying flat on my back trying to stay right in the middle of the bed because I don't want to seem like I'm is favoring either of them.

Matthew turns off the lights, and I listen to the rustling of clothing. I don't dare look. I'm no virgin, but this is uncharted territory. The two of them slide into the bed and cuddle up to me. My eyes pop wide open because they are most definitely naked.

I have two men in my bed with no clothes on. Oh, fuck me. No! Oh, not ready for that. "Why, um, why are you both naked?"

Fen chuckles. "It's how I sleep. Guessing it is the same for Matthew. They just don't make cute pajamas in our size, you know."

Sighing, I lay here as still as possible, thinking there is no way I am going to be able to sleep like this. And then poof, I'm out like the lights.

Fifteen

Matthew left early to find food for her. I made coffee and am now drinking it in the kitchen when Blaze walks in. She startles when she sees me. I raise my brows and say, "You seem really jumpy."

She says, "Last time something unexpected was at that table, it was Pastor Ward's head hanging over it telling us I needed to go back to the church and bring my friends too. You'd be jumpy about that table and things unexpected, too."

I nod, "Fair enough. I would likely feel some kind of way about that, too."

She gets her coffee and is just leaning against the counter drinking it and looking like a whole meal. I need to let her drink her coffee, so I ask her, "When do you need to be at work?"

She says, "I'll just ride with Falina. She is right down the road and will be going in the same time as me, anyway.

Besides, are you both really sure you are ok with this? I know you have issues with Odin. I'm surprised you are willing to go along with anything that creepy old fucker wants you to do."

Standing and walking over, I put my cup in the sink. Leaning in really close to her, it thrills me when her breath catches. My face next to hers and my lips near her ear, I say, "I don't care what Odin wants. I want you. However, that happens. As it stands, though, I am the one person Odin fears. If he bothers you again, I'll take care of it. And I will be taking you to work today."

She swallows and puts a hand on my chest to push me back. "He was just gross and trying to see my boobs. He quit when Hera told him she would be seeing his wife soon."

Her statement draws my eyes down to her breasts, and I drag them back to her face. "How are you today, with the shit your grandmother is doing?"

She shrugs, "As okay as I can be. I hate it. I hate knowing that I'll see more bodies. Hate it that I can't just tell someone and let them deal with it. That I am the one that has to find a way to stop her. I hate that I am so confused about everything right now. That I feel like I must be evil or bad in some way, if not because I want desperately to have the both of you, then because I am descended from her. What if the terrible that is her is in me, too?"

I gently take her cup from her and set it on the counter to the side. Putting my hands on her waist, I lift her up onto the counter. Her legs spread and allow me to stand between them. Gods, I love that. Lifting one hand, I put a finger under her chin and tell her, "You aren't evil. You are good right to your core and that is why they wanted to use you to control us. You would do what is right for the world. No matter how it hurt you, and we're going to work on that part. You won't be stopping your grandmother alone. What the gods didn't count on is how much fire is in your soul. They won't be expecting the defiance that I know they will be getting." The scent of her arousal is inspiring me as I put my hands on the counter to either side of her and lean in, forcing her to lean back. She is breathing heavily and I say, "We could start reminding you of your feral nature right now."

She moans low in her throat and her lips part just as the front door opens and Matthew calls out, "I brought food."

I kiss her neck and back up, saying, "Your timing is shit, Matthew."

Blaze picks up her coffee as she chuckles, content to stay on the counter while I readjust because every part of me is on fire for her.

Blaze

Matthew smirks as he enters the kitchen. He walks over and gives me a kiss, "Good morning love, I brought you food. Are you ok to sit at the table and eat?"

"Yes, I can sit there." Fen looks a little sad as I hop down from the counter. That man has me hot and now I have to sit between the two of them like my panties aren't wet and eat a normal meal.

Matthew sets out the food and Fen grabs plates. He didn't even ask me where they were, he just checked cabinets till he found them. God damn, this stuff is sexy as hell and not helping the state of my panties. We settle around the table and it is excellent. He bought from First Watch. The food there is very good though I haven't been there much because it has been out of my price range, mostly.

My thoughts turn back to my grandmother as I eat. Taking another sip of my coffee, I tell the guys, "My grandmother has to be stopped. If only because I don't need the drinking problem that is rapidly developing from continuing to see her victims."

The guys are silent while I process. I'm not delusional enough to think they are silent because they don't have opinions. I know they are trying to let me work out how I feel like it should be handled before they add their thoughts. "I want Falina and Frankie here while we figure this out. Maybe Glenda too, if she has time." Pulling my phone out of my pajama pocket, I send text messages to them, asking if they could come over to plan with me. Both immediately send back that they will be here soon.

I stand, "I'll be back. I need to get dressed before they get here."

Fen asks, "Would you like some help? Those pajamas look tricky to get out of."

Matthew says, "I would be happy to assist in whatever way you allow."

I stop at the kitchen doorway, turning to look at them. "Thank you, but I think I can handle this."

They laugh as I leave the kitchen and go into my bedroom to change. I close the door because I am still feeling weird about the whole thing. I know I'll get right with it eventually, but today isn't that day. Today, I need to focus on what to do about my grandmother. Grabbing a pair of yoga pants and a t-shirt along with fresh underclothes, I am quickly dressed. Feeling better able to handle the world now that I am dressed, I go back to the kitchen. Sitting down and picking up my fork, I say, "While we are waiting... we need to talk about this." I use the fork as a pointer to indicate the three of us.

Both of them are very interested in hearing what I have to say about it. "I am torn. I want you both and I am concerned that there is another one of you out there based on what Glenda saw. I'm already worried that there is at the very least a seed of evil in me from my grandmother. Plus, I feel a way about the gods wanting to use me like this. It's rude and I fucking want to spite them. And that makes me wonder if I am already a little evil with wanting to spite the gods."

Then Hera pops in standing in the middle of the kitchen and for just a moment, I think my heart stopped entirely as she said, "You aren't evil."

The coffee I threw at the sound of another person in the room hits the wall and shatters into a thousand or so pieces, the last of my coffee splashing much farther that I thought that amount could. Taking a breath, I say, "Jesus fucking christ, you can't just pop in here like that. I am not ok with random pop ins happening in this kitchen." My hand goes to my heart that is racing still. Holy shit, I did not need a heart attack this morning, but here we are and I feel real fucking close to one.

Hera just looks at the coffee. "Your aim needs improvement."

Matthew snickers, "Always good to see you, Hera. Blaze, let me get you some more coffee."

"Yes, thank you Matthew. And thank you Fen for cleaning my mess. Let me help with the glass. Glenda taught me a spell for that. Just hold the dustpan out in front of you." He does what I asked and I recite the words in my head, snapping my fingers to activate the spell. Glenda said it would be much more impressive that way and she's right. I watch as the shards lift and float gently over to the dustpan, settling in without a sound.

Hera smiles at the magic and tells me, "You aren't evil. You are in an irregular situation. So, let me help. First, Sophia doesn't have a single problem with people being with whoever makes them happy. Second, that religion built around her was created by a bunch of men that wanted to get rich and control everyone. They started out with the rule that sex was not allowed and was a sin. They changed it because they realized that the entire religion would die out fast if they didn't. They are not the ones to listen to about who you love or have sex with. I can assure you, your desire to have two or more men is neither evil nor is it new. I suggest you look up the term polyamory and let go of the morality around sex and love. Beyond that, you all will need the connection that is possible if you allow it. Your grandmother is a formidable opponent."

Bile rises in my throat and I struggle to swallow it

down before I ask, "Who is Sophia? Do you know what my grandmother has been doing?"

"I forget the churches tell you all such nonsense. Sophia is the one you all tend to refer to as God. As for your grandmother, I know she has been stealing power, but she works hard to keep us from seeing her."

Sixteen

BLAZE

Accepting the coffee from Matthew, I tell Hera, "She is murdering women for their power. They have been coming to the mortuary. The women are mutilated and I can smell her magic on them. She carves symbols into their bodies to steal their power. The way she is doing it, it is meant to last into their next lives. To drain them in their future. I've been working with Falina to cut the ties to her on these women. It's exhausting, but my control on my fire is getting really good."

Hera pales at my words. "I need to go check some things." She looks at Matthew and Fen, "You need to get rid of the Pastor. He is an annoyance and a distraction. We can't afford it right now."

They look shocked. Matthew says, "You want us to just kill him?"

Fen asks, "Won't that just martyr him?"

Hera nods, "Yes, I want him dead. Who cares if he is a martyr? Dead men don't become gods. No one else has amassed the following he has. He has been broadcasting to millions on a regular basis, convincing them to pray to him. And he is setting up acolytes." She points at me. "Your ex, James, is one of them. With him gone, you both can set your companies to dismantling his and be done with him. The various churches will still need taken care of, but they aren't nearly the threat that Pamela presents. She dove into evil a very long time ago and found depths that many didn't know existed. If I had realized she was killing women for their power, I would have started moving sooner. Get rid of him and make sure she is protected." She points at me again. Then, turning to look directly at me, she says, "Blaze, you don't know enough to go up against her yet. This was a depth none of us were aware she had found. I may have underestimated her power. Do not go up against her personally. Her minions, fine. She's never been one to share power."

Hera poofs out, leaving us very confused. Matthew looks at Fen. "What are we going to do with Blaze while we take care of the pastor?"

Fen shrugs, "I mean, we could take her with us?"

Matthew comes back with, "No, what if her grandmother shows up? We can just run and she won't bother with us so much. It's Blaze she wants."

That's when I speak up, "You aren't doing anything with me. I already called everyone, we'll just change the location to Glenda's and I'll go there. We are going to talk about the problem that is my grandmother. Obviously my training needs to be fast tracked. I am going to change plans for today. Matthew, I'm going to call in today and so is Falina. Please make sure we don't get fired about this."

Standing, I take my coffee with me to the bedroom, where I sit on my bed to make calls to change plans.

Matthew

Shaking my head, I murmur, "I love it when she does that."

Fen says, "Wait till I remind her of her feral side, then you'll see some real fireworks."

Laughing, I tell him, "I don't think she needs you to remind her. We need to find out where the good pastor is. He hasn't been following his routine for the past few days, or perhaps he has been evading the cameras I set up. Whatever it is, I haven't been seeing him."

Fen shrugs. "My network has. He changed his routes because he has a new girlfriend. This one is a witch. I wonder if she is part of the grandmother's group? I haven't checked into her at all. I suppose it won't matter too much as long as we don't eliminate him at her house."

Frowning, I say, "Let's hope not. You have a network here?"

Fen gets up, saying, "I have a network anywhere there are unhoused people. It's work they can do without all the normal job requirements and it gives them money to get out if that is what they choose to do. Plus, the kind of people I watch don't see them. Now I need to collect my clothing." He leaves the room, and I am left thinking about Pastor Ward. Pulling out my phone, I send emails to begin the process of tearing apart the corporations behind his church.

Fen

Leaving Matthew in the kitchen, I take myself off to collect the rest of my clothing from the floor next to Blaze's bed. She is ending a call when I walk in. Her surprise when she sees me walking in has me pointing at my clothing. "I came to get my clothes."

She looks down at them. "Oh, yes. You probably shouldn't wander around without your shirt and shoes. Might be distracting."

She thinks I'm distracting? Good. I was bending down to pick up the shirt when she added the distracting part. I look up to find her staring down at me, looking almost hungry. Shirt in hand, I move closer to where she is sitting on the edge of her bed. "You find me distracting?" She nods, biting her lip. "Considering the day you've had already, maybe a little distraction is just what you need."

Dropping to my knees in front of her, I place my hands carefully to either side of those luscious legs of hers, not actually touching her. Her eyes are focused on my shoulders, her hands curled in her lap as if that is the only way to keep them in place. "My feral wolf, go ahead and be distracted. You are welcome to touch as much or as little as you like. I won't touch you unless you ask me to." Even if it kills me to keep my hands off her.

Her fingers stretch out first. Slowly, her hands move

from her lap to my shoulders. My eyes drift closed as the sensation of her hands on me flows through my body and rights something in me, in my world, that had been off kilter since the day she died.

Her fingers light a trail of fire as they follow the line of my shoulders out and back in toward my neck, trailing down to my pecks where she places her palms flat against my chest, the same way she did before. My eyes fly open, and she is focused on her hands, her face a mask of confusion. She glances up at my eyes and says, "Why do I feel like I've done this before?"

I whisper, "Because you did this at least once a day, before."

She whispers, "I don't think I can stay away from you."

"I'd like it a lot if you didn't."

"What if it destroys your friendship with Matthew?"

"Then we both need to be smacked. And maybe visit a therapist. Because we are both grown and should be able to act like we are."

Her phone rings, and she jumps, her hands leaving my chest. She picks up her phone and, after looking at the screen, she says, "It's Glenda. I need to take this with a focused mind that isn't dwelling in the region of your pectorals."

I laugh as I grab the items I came for and exit the room. Shutting her door behind me, I put on my shirt there in the little hall. I can still feel her hands on my chest. I never thought I would feel that again. How did Matthew survive having been without her for so long? It's only been sixty-ish years for me, though I am a millennium or three older than he is. I've used the hunt to ease the pain, along with joining the Wild Hunt occasionally. I don't know if I would have survived if it had taken that long to see her again. Keeping my shoes in my hand, I head back to the kitchen. Maybe I'll ask Matthew one day while we are drinking.

Seventeen

My mind is still half on the deja vu feeling from my hands on Fen's pecs as Matthew drives me over to Glenda's place. Matthew reaches over and runs a finger down the side of my face. "You're a million miles away. Is everything ok?"

Leaning into his hand, I tell him, "Yes, just a weird sense of déjà vu. I've gotten it with you before, but never so strongly."

He nods. "That is reasonable. We lived hundreds of years ago, around eight hundred of them ago. Your life with Fen was much more recent." Matthew puts his hand back on the steering wheel as he takes a corner.

"Oh. I didn't know that. How did you know? Did you know that me?"

"No, Fen backed away from all of this for the most part. We heard from him and saw him occasionally, but he kept you separate. He always said he didn't want his feral wolf to be tainted by the church."

"I wonder how he feels about that now?"

He stops the car in front of Glenda's place, Fen's bike stops behind us. "If I had to guess, probably that keeping you away from the church is always the right idea. For now, we have a pastor to eliminate and you have magic to learn. Can I have a kiss before you go?"

I turn to face him and lean in. As always, when our lips touch, it's electric. His arms circle me and I am half in his lap before I realize what's happening. I could stay here forever, safe in his arms. We break the kiss and I put my forehead against his. "This, this is when I get the déjà vu with you. My forehead against yours, it feels like I've done this a million times, but maybe it was a dream."

Matthew says, "It wasn't a dream. You did this every time we kissed. You said you were making sure we stayed connected."

I sit back, worming my way back into my seat and realizing my shirt is not where I left it. As I fix that, I say, "I guess it worked, because here we are. Connected in another life."

"Indeed, it did." He gets out of the car while I get my clothing situated and walks around to my door, opening it as the last of it is back in place. His hands are fast. I didn't realize how much he had done while we were kissing.

He extends a hand to help me out of the car. I take it because it is sweet and I enjoy the display of chivalry from a man that would do anything to keep me happy. He tugs me to him and kisses me again. I am left breathless and more than a little needy feeling as he says, "I love you. Stay safe."

"I love you, come back safe."

He turns and nods at Fen before he gets in his car and drives away.

I walk over to Fen and tell him, "Come back safe, ok?"

He smirks at me, "Interested in my return?"

Shrugging, I say, "I never said I wasn't interested. I'm just conflicted about it."

Fen grins at me, "Want a little help deciding?"

Tipping my head a little, I say, "Ok?"

There is no time to react as he stands and his arms shoot out, snatching me to him, pressing my body against his. He inhales my scent, his nose moving along the line of delicate, warm flesh from my shoulder and up my neck. One hand moves up and grabs a fistful of my hair, turning my face up to his.

His lips touch mine and it feels like he just claimed me. The kiss is deep and fire and wakens every nerve ending. I am lost in him when he breaks the kiss and sets me back on the sidewalk. He holds my arms until I am steady again. As the haze clears from my mind he says, "Go on in there, I'll see you soon. We need to get rid of this guy so he is one less worry for you."

I nod, "Yes, come back safe." He grins as I turn and walk toward the house. When I reach the door, I turn and wave before going in. Gods, these men are going to drive me to distraction is what they are going to do. How am I supposed to think about magic when all I have on my mind is the two of them?

And little flashes of memories that didn't happen in this life.

Fen

I wave back at her and watch till she closes the door. The second the door closes, I reach down readjust myself. That's better. I think I was cutting off circulation or something. Fuck all these shitty religions and their hangups about sex. And fuck all the gods for setting her up like this.

Starting my bike again, I head for the place we agreed to meet at. It's a parking area for a small, upscale park. The kind where white ladies run thinking it is a safe place. They never even notice the unhoused ones hiding in the darker parts. I'm ready to go, but we can't do this at the mistress's house. I think we could have if we brought Blaze, but that is not just my decision. So now we are both leaned against Matthew's car when he asks, "How did it go saying goodbye to her?"

I smile, thinking of it. "She allowed me a kiss."

Matthew looks away for a moment. When he looks back, he says, "I'm happy for you. I don't really like it yet, but I am happy for you. I remember the joy you had during the times that I spoke to you while you were with her."

"I was happy, probably for the first time in over a thousand years. I know it will be different this time. I'm ok with that because maybe this time she'll get to live. Maybe between us we can keep her alive."

Matthew nods. "Nothing takes the soul out of you quite like a mate dying. Hell, that's how I ended up here."

"My reason wasn't so noble. Freya begged me to put things aside and help this cause while she convinced Odin to let go of that foolish belief. I don't care if he never lets go of it but Freya is a good person. I figured I'd at least not be bored."

Matthew laughs. "As reasons go, it isn't the worst."

The preacher steps out of his girlfriend's front door. Hot damn. Hopefully, he will go home now. Matthew follows him and I head for a convenience store near his house. The unhoused that hang out here recognize me. As I'm greeting them, Matthew messages to let me know the pastor is home. We wait for night to fall. Matthew in his car and me hanging with the unhoused people. I buy them food and beer; we talk about things while we eat. By the time we've finished eating, it's dark. Matthew messages again, saying that he will wait by the back door. I tell the unhoused guys that I have to go take care of some business and I will give them each a twenty when I get back if they keep people away from my bike. They are happy to help and most of them say they would do it for free because I already paid them in food and beer. I'm giving them the cash, anyway.

I walk off into the darker spaces, where the little wild that remains in this place offers enough shadow to keep me unseen as I shift.

I smell the disturbance in the neighborhood smells long before I arrive at the back door of the pastor's home. It has the fur along my spine raised and a low growl emanating from my chest as I draw near. It's a trap. How did he find out we were coming tonight?

Eighteen

BLAZE

I am still dazed as I close the door behind me. Falina is standing off to the left. She's been watching through the window the whole time. The minute the door is closed she says, "Girl. What are you doing? The vampire *and* the wolf? What are you thinking?"

I tell her the short and still wild version of things. She is just as stunned as I am. Finally she says, "I guess at least they gave you the hot, powerful ones. And really, high five for having two of them. Keep me in the loop. I need to live vicariously through you. The rest of the dating pool is heavily polluted."

"You want details? Really?"

"I do, girl. I can't even find myself a single one to bump uglies with. You have two. I definitely want details. And if they have friends, I would not be averse to some ancient evil that wants to throw my back out nightly and treat me like his queen. To clarify, I'm pan, so it really doesn't matter the gender of the friend."

"In that case, last night I was upset, you know, from work." She nods, a look of deep sadness flashing across her face before she masks it again. "And so Fen found me at the bar, talked with me and brought me home. Then the two of them crawled into bed and slept next to me, naked. I didn't think I would be able to sleep with all that on either side of me. I did, passed right out. But damn."

Falina laughs and says, "Oh! Frankie is already in the room with Grams. We should get in there. I got distracted with all the making out on the sidewalk. You really fell asleep between the two of them?"

"Yeah. I don't know if it was the shots or emotional exhaustion, but next thing I knew, it was morning and they were both already out of the bed."

We go in and over half the family is in there already. Grams sees us enter and calls everyone to quiet down as we move to stand next to Frankie. The next hour is a large protection casting. I've never had the opportunity to be part of a group working and this is amazing. I can feel the magic of all the women and men in the room. Our magics are flowing in and around each other as we cast this large protective spell, and this is the most magical I have ever felt in my life.

We finish the spell and I feel almost high from the magic still present in the room. Snacks and drinks are being brought out, Falina tells Frankie and me, "We'll all need to eat and drink to ground after that big a working."

I ask, "Is that why I feel a little high?"

She giggles, "That's a pretty accurate description of the feeling. Yes, it is."

One of the women comes through handing out drinks.

As I take mine, we hear the doorbell ring and the house shakes. I look at Glenda and she closes her eyes a moment. When she opens them, she announces, "We are under attack. Pamela's minions are here."

Oh fuck. How did they know I'm here?

Matthew

I can smell the other humans in the house when I get to the back of the house. The fools have left the lights on, so they are easy to see as I hover near the windows. It looks to be at least ten in the rooms near the back of the house. They are sitting around tables and on couches. Relaxed. Moving around the house, I notice the windows at the front of the house are dark. The curtains drawn. Ah, they expect us to come in through the front door. Heading for the back door, I get there just before Fen. He is sniffing the air and the ground. He whines softly and looks toward the back door as I materialize near him.

"I know. Fen, it's up to you. I feel like we can take them from what I have seen. There are probably twenty to thirty people in there. At least. But we know it's meant to be an ambush. We can come back another night. Do you smell any magic here?"

Fen shakes his great big wolf head. "Good, because that is the one thing they haven't figured out how to hide. I didn't smell anything either. It's your call. Do we stay or go?"

He stares at the door for some time and I wonder, as I

have since I met him, what magics might he have inherited from his parents? He snorts and gestures toward the door with his nose.

I ask him, "So we are staying?"

He nods and walks toward the door. All right. Here we go. A couple steps have me next to him and I use my vampire magic to make sure the door isn't locked. Kicking it down is such a waste of a good surprise. Turning the knob, I give the door a little push inward and let it swing open.

Nineteen

MATTHEW

The men in the kitchen don't even turn to look as we walk in. I pull out the knife I keep in a hidden pocket of my pants. Using my speed, I run around the table in a blur, slicing the throats of the men sitting there. By the time I stop, the first one has begun to gurgle. Grinning with pleasure at my kills, I turn to Fen. He rolls his eyes and uses a paw to point, first at me and the front of the house. Then at the next room and himself. I nod and head for the front of the house. Becoming less corporeal allows blending with the shadows better as I traverse the hallway. I'm about half down the hall when the fight starts behind me.

The screams are loud and I'm not the only one that hears it. Men start running toward me. I stab the first one, driving my knife up from his belly to puncture his diaphragm and one of the lungs supported by it. The second one tries to run past his friend, but I punch him in the throat. My hands fly, killing one after the other. I can hear the sounds of Fen in the other room, in between the screams of his victims.

I suppose I would scream too if a wolf that much bigger than any other wolf in existence walked into the room and set to killing everyone. I finish off the last of the men running toward the sound of Fen's attack and move to the end of the hall. I round the corner into a room and a gun fires. The bullet goes straight through;, it hurts like hell and pisses me off. Flying across the room, I leap over the couch and grab the man as I roll. He fires two more shots into me before I snap his neck. I hear Fen pad into the room while I am laying there letting the wounds heal.

He transforms and says, "You let him shoot you three times? You're getting slow."

Lifting one hand, I curl it into a fist as I raise my middle finger at him. He laughs and says, "Come on, we need to finish this. Can't be leaving witnesses to a wolf and a man taking out a house full of people."

Twenty

Blaze

There are children in the house, and their moms are
more than a little terrified for them. The room is filled with
discussions and fear when Glenda projects her voice to
say, "Quiet! We are not defeated nor will we be." The
room quiets, with the exception of a couple of people
sniffling. "The ones with children here, you and the
children, will leave via the tunnel. Everyone else, you are
with me. We are going outside and show them exactly why
Pamela has left us alone all these years."

The fear in the room recedes, as we are all given things
to do. Glenda calls over those of us with the more
elemental powers. There are five of us. Two with fire
counting myself, Frankie with air, Falina with earth, and
another woman with water. Glenda tells us, "You all are
going to be the offense with me. We are aiming to kill.
These women are not here to teach us a lesson, they are
here to end us. The only mercy you may offer them is a

quick death. Are we clear? Can you handle this? Speak now if you cannot."

The image of the woman I burned to death flashes through my mind. I look at the faces of the people surrounding me; the father saying goodbye to his wife and child before they leave. The women in a small circle amping up for defense. I can't let them down. Looking back at Glenda, I nod, shoving the image of that woman I killed with fire away. Glenda nods and walks over to the small circle. She talks to them briefly, then says to us all, "Let's go."

As we near the front door, we can hear shots slamming into the shield. Glenda laughs. "That shield was created hundreds of years ago and strengthened by every witch born into this family. They won't break through it that way. At least, not within the next year, if they could keep it up for that long. It absorbs the energy thrown at it. All right, offense to the front, defense stays behind the shield."

We file out the front door and stand shoulder to shoulder, waiting long enough to allow for the defense witches to get us protected. The women stop firing at the shield, one of them shouts at us, "About time you cowards came out to face us! Give us the half breed and we'll let you live."

My heart freezes in my chest. I knew they came for me. What did I ever do to my grandmother to cause her to hate me like this? Their faces are shadowed with the twilight. Even with the outside lights turned on, they are still just outside the reach of the light. I wonder if that is by design? Would I recognize them if they stepped into the light and let us see their faces? Glenda laughs, "Pamela still desperate for power? Did she ever start sharing it? Or has she left you with just your own powers, only a little depleted as part of your fealty to her?"

The one that shouted at us snarls, "What would you know about our high priestess? The offer is rescinded. You and everyone here will die for your insolence."

The women fire at us. I flinch at the first few that hit just a few inches from me. The only one that doesn't is Glenda. Balls of steel on that woman as she fires off a shot. The woman dodges it and keeps firing at us. I throw fireballs at them. They are fast. Then Falina and the water witch work together and create a muddy morass under their feet. Frankie uses the air to knock the women back toward our shots and one of Glenda's shots hits. I am going to have to be better than they are, have to be able to protect my men while I attack. Fuck.

The woman she hit stops in her tracks and collapses. Glenda is looking tired. Fuck, I can't have her hurt to protect me. I double my efforts, firing shots like mad. I see them hitting, but the fire isn't killing them fast. I heat up the balls, so they are like magma. Firing those does a lot more damage. The screams of the woman I hit in the forehead are horrific, but I keep going.

Our shields are faltering. We've taken too long. I see the leader taking aim at Glenda, and I leap in front of her. The shot hits me in the shoulder and it hurts. Oh fucking hell, does it hurt. Then the earth under the woman becomes liquid, and she drops like a stone. Only her hand makes it back out before it solidifies. There are still two left. They are both looking at the other witches still standing, firing at them. Using the hand that isn't feeling real fucking painful, I fire off another one of the magma balls at one. It hits and she screams. Looking at me, she screeches, "You've only made her more powerful. You'll die in pain."

She falls to the ground as her friend is hit and falls next to her. Her eyes are vacant but still seem focused on me. Dragging my eyes from the macabre sight, I struggle with getting up when one side of my upper body is on fire with pain.

Frankie helps me up and Falina rushes in, hugging me hard. She whispers, "Thank you. Thank you. Thank you. We need her so much."

The hug is hurting my shoulder. The pain is excruciating. I'm trying to bear it, but Glenda sees my face and says, "Falina, you're hurting her. Let her go so we can get her taken care of."

As she releases me, I grit out, "I need to call my brother. I promised I would call him if anything happened."

Frankie pulls my phone out of my back pocket. "Unlock it and I'll call him."

I tell her to hold it up in front of my face and I school my features to the expression it will accept. It unlocks and I can hear her talking to Chad as Glenda looks at my shoulder. She says, "Falina, call Linna back. Tell her the fighting is over and we need her to help pull this out."

I'm a little concerned about how she phrased that. "Pull what out?"

"Just a spell. What she hit you with was pretty nasty. But we'll get it out and you'll be fine."

"What happens if you don't get it out?"

She sighs, "Nothing good, nothing at all good. Let's not talk about this where Falina can hear, ok?"

I nod as Falina comes over, "Frankie says your brother is on the way. He says you are not to move until he gets here. And that if you die, he is going to have us bring you back so he can kick your ass."

I laugh and groan. "Is Linna nearly here?" My shoulder is throbbing ever harder with the pain. Frankie seems to still be messaging on my phone. Oh geez, she is probably telling Matthew and Fen. Just what I need. They weren't overly keen on today's plan to begin with and only really went along with not hiding me away because I said I was coming here to train.

Falina is studying my shoulder intently. She says, "Yes, she was ten minutes out. She should get here soon. And everyone else will probably get here in time to be a pain in the ass while she is fixing you."

I can see it on her face when she realizes what the spell I took in Glenda's place is, when the horror of how close she came to losing her sets in. A hand goes to her mouth and her eyes squeeze shut. Frankie comes over and turns her away, walking her towards the house as she tells her, "Don't think about what could have been. It isn't. Your grandmother is whole and safe, and we'll make sure she stays that way."

Falina throws her arms around Frankie and cries, "I don't want Blaze to be hurt, either. I can't lose either of them."

Frankie hugs her tightly. "You won't be losing anyone. We're going to get rid of those bitches. Just you watch and see." Frankie's eyes meet mine and I nod. We are going to get rid of them. My grandmother cannot be allowed to take Glenda from us. And I don't think I could do this without my friends, so I'm going to have to be able to protect a crowd. I can't lose them.

Twenty-One

We split up to search the rest of the house. Matthew takes the upstairs and I head for the basement, shifted back into my wolf form. Keeping an ear out for anything, I pad down the stairs. The basement area seems fairly empty. Except for this odd smell. It's not a drug. It seems familiar somehow. Rounding a corner, I recognize the smell as my eyes land on a bomb. Son-of-a-bitch. I freeze in place, looking around for any way that I might trip the damn thing. The wires on it lead across the room and, oh fuck me. Turning, I run for the stairs, howling. Praying that Matthew doesn't trip anything on the way, since those wires lead up toward the second floor through the stairs. I make it to the first floor the same time Matthew does and I bark at him as I keep running for the back door.

We won't die, but regenerating from a bomb would hurt like hell.

Matthew is right behind me as I clear the door and

keep going. The night lights up as the force of the explosion throws us.

I hit someone's wall and fall to the ground. Fuck, this guy is going to die slow. I shift while I'm laying there. The shift helps the healing process along, though it hurts a lot fucking more to shift while injured. Luckily, I had a lot of practice ignoring pain with Odin's bullshit, so I make the shift with my jaw clenched.

Sitting up still isn't the most pleasant thing, but I can. My ribs feel like I was kicked. So does the rest of me. But nothing seems to be in the wrong place, so that's a relief. Putting bones back where they belong is not something I can do quietly. Looking around, I spot Matthew getting to his feet. He comes limping over and offers a hand. I take it, because these ribs are not happy with me already.

He says, "How did you know?"

"Found the bomb, saw the wires leading up. Fuck this guy. I want to bite him."

Matthew laughs, "Me too."

Our phones both ping. I pull mine out and it's from Blaze. Opening the message, I see that it's Falina on her phone. They were attacked. How did they know? A bomb here, an attack on her there. This is no coincidence. A message from Matthew pings in,

Matthew: Is Blaze safe?

Falina: Yes. She's injured, but we are fixing that.

Me: Still where we dropped her off?

Falina: Yes.

Matthew: We're on our way

Matthew asks me, "Want a ride to your bike?"

"No, I'm good. See you there." It hurts like hell, but I take off running. I know I'll be fully healed by the time I get to her. What's a little pain if it gets me to her?

Twenty-Two

MATTHEW

Thank fuck she is ok. I don't understand how they knew. Getting to my car is slower than I would like. The healing process is fast, but it still takes a little time. One of my legs hit something or got hit and it hurts like hell. Making it to the car, I find a note.

Snatching it off my windshield, I open it.

Matthew,

So sorry to have missed you. Hope my little surprise was exciting enough for you. Too bad you couldn't save her this time, either.

W

They knew. These motherfuckers knew we would be splitting up. Knew where she would be. But how? Crumpling the note in my hand I get in the car and toss it over to the passenger seat. I need to get to her now. She is their target. We are just in the way.

As I try to get in the car, I realize there is something in my leg. Straightening, I twist to see the back of my thigh.

A fairly large chunk of wood is sticking out of my leg. Well, no wonder it still hurts so much. I can hear sirens as I snatch it out, pressing a fist to my mouth to hold back the scream. Fuck this guy. Pastor Ward is going to die painfully. Tossing the wood into the back seat, I get in my car. My leg feels so much better already.

The drive through town gives me time to process. I don't see how they could have known unless someone told them and that someone had to know things we didn't tell anyone. But how? Are they scrying? How do we defend against that? Did they find some way to tell the future?

Pulling up to the Glenda's house, the place looks like a war zone. The front yard is a mess of char and what looks like it was mud. There is a hand sticking up out of the ground. Fen just got off his bike, and he gives the hand a nudge as he walks past. It doesn't move much.

Putting the car in park and shutting it off, I head across the yard to where Chad is hovering over Blaze and the woman working on her. Fen's fists are clenched and as I lean to see the shoulder that is being worked on, I see bone. That's no minor injury. They almost got her. We left her and they almost got her. Tapping Fen, I ask him, "Did you get a note?"

He reaches into a pocket and hands me a crumpled ball of paper, never taking his eyes off Blaze. Smoothing it out, I find the exact same note as I found. Fen says, "The people I had watching my bike told me that a car pulled up about a minute after I left and gave them the note for me. How did they know, Matthew?"

Hera appears near Blaze. The woman working on Blaze is visibly tiring as Hera touches her forehead with one finger. The woman glows and Blaze heals fast. Both sides of her flesh growing towards each other as we watch.

Hera looks over at us and says, "I don't know who, yet. We have a traitor in our midst. Someone that has inside information. I have suspicions but nothing concrete yet. None of these people can see me. They don't know I am here. Just you two and Blaze as she comes out of the haze of pain. I don't have more information right now. Don't talk about anything out loud and if you are thinking about writing it down, don't. Wait until I contact you again. I know the Pastor Ward is still alive. We'll deal with him soon enough." She looks down and sees Blaze's shoulder is nearly healed. Removing her finger from the woman's forehead she tells us, "I will come see you soon. Trust no one."

Her message delivered, she disappears. The woman healing Blaze says, "Holy shit. That was insane."

Glenda asks, "What do you mean?"

She says, "I was exhausted. I thought we were going to need to call in someone else. Then it was like I got the fastest recharge ever. When I opened my eyes, the healing was nearly finished."

Glenda looks hard at Blaze. She shrugs. Glenda doesn't look even a little convinced, but she lets it go. The witches start cleaning up, making the yard look like it did before. Someone makes the hand sink into the ground, for which I am grateful. I am fine with tearing people to bits, killing them. No problem with any of that. But leaving the hand sticking out like that was giving me the creeps.

Blaze

We left Chad, Matthew, and Fen in the living area while we went back to the ritual room to rework a few things. All of us are tired, well, except Linna. She needs the grounding she'll get when someone hands her a cookie. Inside, Glenda says, "I'm not asking what exactly happened. I know there is a reason you didn't say. Gods know I've had my own moments like that. What I want is for you to promise not to take Pamela on by yourself."

Guilt races through me, and I look at Falina. She shakes her head no. I raise my brows and frown. She hangs her head briefly, saying, "Go ahead, she will not be happy I didn't tell her."

Glenda sighs. "What have you two been hiding?"

"Pamela has been killing other witches to steal their power. The spell she is using, it's vile. It follows them into the next life."

Glenda says, "I see. What have you two been doing when you find these women?"

Falina says, "We've been removing it, un-linking the women, and Blaze has been cremating them herself. That's why she has been doing all the extra practice we talked about."

Glenda nods. "That explains why your fire control is so much better. It wasn't just to practice. You felt it must be done. There was no choice for you. It wasn't one or two of them, was it?"

"No. Lately it has been one or two minimum, per day. I needed to make sure it stuck. I couldn't let those women suffer in their next lives, too."

Glenda nods. "You are much more powerful than any of us guessed. That fight we were just in, it lasted maybe fifteen minutes. Our shield people were faltering when we finished. They aren't weak. But holding things for periods of time like that is difficult. It requires a well of power that many of us do not have access to, ever. This is why your grandmother was so desperate to keep you from realizing your power. Why she is now so interested in taking control of you, of your power. Whatever you must do, don't let her take you. If you have to murder your way through her coven, you don't worry about it. You are stopping her from becoming the most powerful evil in this world."

"What? No. You're joking right? If she gets me she becomes the most powerful?"

"The most powerful evil, yes. Do you know what makes a person evil?"

"Their actions. Committing sins and going against the gods."

"No. Sin is a human construct and the gods are as fickle and contrary as we are. Our actions play a part in it. However, the intent behind the actions, the why; it plays as much a part as the action itself. For instance, we killed today. We did so in self defense. There is no stain on us for the deaths of those women. Pamela, she has been killing for power since she was very young. The deaths she has caused over the years have stained her soul darker and darker over the years till nothing remains of her former self."

"How do you know so much about her?"

"We were friends once, childhood friends. She wasn't evil then. She was just a child with a terrible mother. Her mother hated her. We'll never know why. Her death wasn't Pamela's first kill, but it may have been where she got her lust for power from."

"She killed her own mother? That's horrible."

Glenda sighs, "It's more complicated than it seems. Pamela's mother was a horrible person. She abused her children. Honestly, Pamela was a favorite until her little brother was born. That was when the change started. She has an older sister who is powerful in her own right but never traveled the dark paths that Pamela has been drawn to walking. You look a lot like her. Your mother does too, though not so much as you. Pamela tormented everyone in the family and was miserable to many people outside the family from a young age. At the same time, small animals had accidents around her. The older she got, the less anyone could trust her. Too many terrible injuries happened when there were no witnesses. Her mother encouraged all this. As Pamela displayed more evil, her mother would give her little bits of attention as a reward for her deeds. Only when the brother wasn't around, mind you. Then she caught her mother fighting with her father. Heard her say terrible things about her. She was distraught at first. Then she decided her mother had to pay."

Glenda sighs, looking at a painting on the wall. The painting is curious, being a landscape that looks a bit like a face. "Her evil has grown by leaps and bounds since then. Don't stare at the painting for too long dear, it isn't healthy."

I pull my eyes from the painting, and she continues. "She chose her path. The sister, their mother, abused her much worse and yet, she is nothing like Pamela. All this is to say that evil is a choice, and you can always choose. Even now, Pamela could choose better. She would have much to make up for, but she could choose differently."

"I have a grand-aunt out there somewhere?"

"Well, hmm, technically, she would be your grandmother. Pamela did not give birth to your mother. She manipulated her and uses her to hurt her sister."

"What? You're joking. She's the grand aunt?"

"Yes. Jealousy is a terrible thing."

"Are you still in contact with her? If she is the opposite of the woman I knew as my grandmother, I want to know her."

Glenda frowns. "I do still know her. She has cut off the rest of the family, she couldn't take the lies and the hurt. I will ask her if she is willing to meet you. I can't promise anything more than that."

"If you think it will help, you are welcome to tell her anything you know about me. Having a family is nice and I would welcome more. And there's Chad too. He is her grandson. I think he would like to meet her as well."

Chad called brother privilege to get to take me home once I finished at Glenda's for the day. He sent Fen and Matthew for coffee and food, telling them I would need those to keep up my strength after all that had happened today. They were both fully aware that he was claiming some time with his sister and allowed it. They were not happy about it. I think Fen may have been growling as he left. I know Matthew was grumbling. They both came to kiss me before they left on their errands.

I am entirely amused by the reactions; they are sweet. Chad and I get in his car, the drive to my house is short. He is quiet for the drive. When we get in the house, he sits on my couch. I sit on the opposite end to wait for him to speak. I know something is on his mind. Then he says, "The family has been talking."

My heart drops out of my chest. They don't want me. I'm too much trouble and they are bowing out. Oh, no. No. Dammit. I just got a family. I thought they cared.

When I don't say anything he continues, "We all want to be more involved in your life. We know you haven't had good family experiences before now, but we can't change that if we don't get the chance. The thing is, the family has been in that area for a long time. We are kind of packed in there."

"Wait, you want to be more involved? You aren't saying goodbye because I'm too much trouble?"

"What? No! No. Not at all."

"I'm going to need a minute to wrap my head around this. I thought you were here to tell me you all were bowing out. I was having a minor panic about this. Just, uh, give me a moment." My heart is still beating so fast. Thank god he isn't laughing at me, that would suck. I'm not sure the concern he has on his face as I take some deep breaths to calm myself is a lot better, but I'll take it. Once I feel less like I am falling apart at the seams, I tell him, "Ok. So you all somehow want to be more involved?"

He smiles, "Yes. We do. And since there is a lot of our family over where we live, it's well past time some of us split off and start another space. We haven't acted on that yet because we wanted to get your ok before we move over this way and start showing up at your house so much more. Before Dad and Leann decide, you need a house on the property. They will find something near you, if you agree to this. Do you have any thoughts about it? Questions?"

Oh boy do I. "Yes, I have a few questions. Why would you all pack up and move here for me? You barely know me. Maybe I'm a monster in disguise. Don't you all have roots there? Lives? It isn't that far away. I don't want to pull you all away from that. Would I love having you closer? Yes. But I can't ask that of you all. Especially with the danger. There are people, our grandmother and her coven, to be specific, trying real hard to kill me. You all coming closer will put you all back in her crosshairs."

Before Chad can respond, Matthew and Fen walk in with food and coffee. I don't often drink coffee at night, but I can't say I'm sad to have some on this night. We follow them to the kitchen and Matthew unpacks a feast while Fen pulls out a large thermos of coffee, to-go cups, and a variety of additives.

Never in my life have I had anyone go to these lengths to ensure I have what I need. They tell me to sit while they do this and Chad grabs plates and utensils. Never again will I allow someone's awful son to treat me so bad. Who cares what I think I deserve? I won't accept less than what these two men are doing. Everything is finally laid out and food on everyone's plates, we start eating.

Matthew brought Indian food. I wonder if he has any idea how much I love paneer? The samosas are amazing. As I dip into containers for a second helping, I realize that everyone else is still on their first. Oh geez, I guess today took more out of me than I thought. Chad fills in the silence, "While you all were fetching this feast, I was talking with Blaze about the family possibly moving closer. She is concerned about us being back in Grandma's crosshairs. What do you all think?"

Fen grins. "I think more wolves in the area can only be a good thing."

Matthew snorts, "I agree that more family would be good for Blaze. But, she isn't wrong. Pamela will be after you all as well. She will not want you supporting her. They tried to get us out of the picture for a long time tonight."

"What? You didn't say anything about that. What happened?"

My breath catches as they tell us about the ambush and the bomb in the pastor's house. "If the bomb had caught you, what would have happened?"

Fen shrugs. "It would have hurt like hell and we would have been sidelined while we regenerated. Probably would have taken a month or more, depending on whether we got to a safe place to heal and rest."

Pinning the two of them with a hard stare, I say, "That's not ok. You are both going to have to be more careful, at least as careful as you want me to be."

Chad laughs, "Anyway, I take it you are in support of the family being closer?"

Fen and Matthew both nod. I shrug. Looking down at my food, I mumble, "I just really don't want to be the reason someone I care about dies. Or gets hurt."

Chad finishes chewing and says, "To be fair, we get into our own messes too. Admittedly, they aren't so strong or so evil as grandmother, but they can be deadly."

"Oh! I forgot, or maybe I just haven't had time to let it all sink in. Pamela isn't technically our grandmother, her older sister is."

Chad drops his fork. "I'm sorry, I don't think I heard you right."

"Oh, you heard me right."

"So Pamela has an older sister, and she somehow took our mother from her and cos-played as her mom? What? Why?"

"I don't know all the details. I just found out this afternoon. I asked Glenda to contact her. See if she would be willing to meet me. I don't know if she will. She apparently cut off the rest of the family."

Chad says, "I can see why she might do that, considering what little I know about that side of the family."

Matthew says, "Are you sure about this? I mean, as awful as Pamela is, she convinced one of the sister's kids to crossover to her. Maybe the sister is worse?"

I shake my head no. "Glenda would have said something if she was worse. She didn't. She said something about her having cut off the family for being terrible and hurtful. I'm not really sure Glenda would have told me about her at all if I hadn't been concerned about being evil myself." All three of them stare at me with raised brows. Keeping from squirming is difficult as I tell them, "Yes, I know. Evil is a choice, and I am not evil by birth. Glenda said similar."

Fen smirks and good god is it sexy. Those broad shoulders, dark hair worn long and brushing his shoulders, the beard and mustache that are both kept short. He looks rough and is the perfect contrast to Matthew's polished look. Matthew has his usual button-up shirt. Today the pants are jeans, but they look like they were brand new this morning. His hair is short and styled. His shoulders aren't quite as broad as Fen's are, but he is no less muscular.

I need to focus. How am I going to manage having two men? "I guess, Chad, if you all really want to, I am for it. I would really love having you all close. But how much space are you going to need for the family? How many are coming? I know I haven't met everyone."

"No, you haven't. Leann and Ell have cousins they share the running of the pack with. They could easily leave a whoever wanted to stay with them and have no worries. Plus, we would have backup that we could call on if we had need. We haven't settled on a spot. We want a fairly large plot of land, preferably backed up to a state park forest. It will probably take some time to find the right place."

Matthew clears his throat. "Unless maybe someone you know happened to have some land that he bought ages ago with vague plans to develop it later. Plans that never actually came to fruition."

"Matthew, are you saying you have a large piece of land that you haven't done anything with?"

He looks away for a moment. "I am. I bought it a few

decades ago, and I had mostly forgotten about it. It's about a hundred acres, a little way from here. I don't know if you noticed, but you live pretty close to the nature preserve. The only thing you all would need to be cautious about is the trail cams. You lot are pretty big, even for wolves. And this lug," he jerks a thumb toward Fen, "is even bigger. If you all don't get those cameras sorted, there will be scientists crawling the area looking for giant wolves."

Chad looks excited. "Are you willing to sell it to us?"

Matthew nods, "Yes. I am happy to. I know you will need to look at it and check things like zoning. I'll give your number to my people and have them fast track it all for you. Whatever you need, and we'll get you all sorted."

Chad says, "I need to pass it on to my aunts. They will make the decisions but I think we would love that. How far away from here did you say it is?"

"Maybe five minutes?"

Chad stands, "Excuse me, I need to call Aunt Leann."

He walks into the other room. I look at Matthew. "Are you sure you want to do this?"

He nods as he picks up a samosa. "Having that family close can only benefit you. I want you happy, safe, and healthy. Them being closer to you works to further all of those goals. The aunts will watch over you, as will your father and brother. They'll be close. All good things."

Fen says, "Full agreement. Wolves need their packs."

Twenty-Three

FEN

It's been a week since we kissed. A week that has been crowded with training and family and learning about her heritage on both sides of the family. Her time has been filled with all those things and work. And with the family working at moving closer, buying the property from Matthew. Apparently, the biggest argument right now is what he will allow them to pay for the property. He wants to charge a rock bottom price and the aunts believe they should pay fair market value.

Matthew and I have barely seen her. Based on the text messages, we don't think it is intentional. She has reached out at least once a day, even if it was long after we already messaged that day. Chad told me she'll be running with the family tonight, and said that if I could get her permission, I could run with them.

So here I am, a little before sunset at her door. She answers quickly and smiles when she sees me. I lift my arms up and out, "Can I have a hug?"

She leaps into my arms, and it is the best feeling to hold her again. When I release her, she takes my hand and draws me into the house. "I haven't gotten to see you much this week. Come sit on the couch with me for a little bit. I can't stay long, but I won't be mad if you are here when I get back."

Sitting down next to her, I slip an arm around her, pulling her in a little closer. "Your brother told me the family is taking you running tonight."

"He did? Wow, he must like you."

"We have a few things in common. He invited me, but said I had to clear it with you first."

She tilts her head to look up at me. "I would love for you to come run with us. I never asked because I'm still new to the family. I don't know what is ok to say. You know? The family I was raised in… there wasn't much safety there. Speaking was always dangerous. Not that silence was safer, but at least I wasn't helping them when I stayed silent. No giving them insights into what I wanted that could be used to hurt me."

Squeezing her a little, I don't know if it is to comfort her or me. "I understand. My family hasn't exactly been what one would call safe either."

"Am I understanding correctly? You are the Fenrir, the one supposed to kill Odin?"

"I am."

"I know the myths say that he kept you locked up, chain around your neck, but that was an exaggeration, right?"

"Unfortunately for me, it was not. If anything, it was too kind to the old bastard."

"Oh no, why are you working with him now?"

I'm saved from answering by her family scratching at the back door. She jumps up and says, "Ready?"

We walk to the back door. When she opens it there are roughly a dozen wolves of various shades ranging from white to black milling about in the yard. Blaze introduces me to the silver one at the door, saying, "Aunt Ell, this is Fen. Fen, this is my Aunt Ell. He is going to run with us tonight. If it's ok?" She nods and Blaze says, "Great. Let's shut this door behind us to keep the spell active all over, and we'll shift outside." The silver wolf turns and walks away from the door as we come out. No sooner than the door is shut, Blaze is changed. Her wolf is white, frosted with silver at the ends of her fur. Opening, I slip into my form. My wolf's form is a little bigger than the others, but I keep it within the size of a regular shifter.

The silver wolf takes the lead and we run. Through the woods and back ways, to another larger, wooded area. Through the mist and moonlight, until she leads us back to Blaze's place as the sky lightens. I can't remember the last time I ran with a pack of wolves. This was… amazing. I wonder if they would let me run with them again?

At Blaze's house, she shifts back into her human form before kneeling to hug the wolves. They each walk over for their hug. The silver one is last, her Aunt Ell. She gives me a sniff as she allows the hug. Her eyes meet mine and she blinks once at me. Then she gives Blaze's face a lick and leads the rest of the pack away.

I feel like her aunt saw much more than I would want her to see. She didn't bare her teeth at me and try to drive me away so I'll take it. Shifting, I follow Blaze in the house. She moves to the sink, starts filling a kettle. I can smell the anxious energy in her.

Leaning against the wall next to the door, I wait. And watch. She bustles around the kitchen. Tidying, making two cups of tea. When there is nothing left to do, she turns and faces me, "I never asked if you want tea. I just made you tea. Do you want tea?"

Crossing the room to her, I take the cup from her. "I will drink tea with you."

Her eyelids drop as a shiver runs through her. I step back with my cup as her eyes open again. I see a little of the wild woman I knew flickering in her eyes and I know she has to be the one to start this. I want that feral wolf woman back. Turning, I walk over to the table and pull out a chair for her. She looks confused as she sits in the chair. It's going to half kill me holding back and waiting for her to find herself.

Twenty-Four

BLAZE

It seems like I spend more time at Glenda's place than anywhere else these days. So when she calls me as I am getting ready for work, I'm not exactly surprised. "What's up Glenda?"

"I have a surprise for you. Could you come over?"

"I was getting ready for work. Is it a now thing or could I come by later?"

"Now, please. You won't want to miss this, and I don't know when I can make it happen again. You can bring your brother if he is available. He would probably be interested in this too."

"Chad? Um, ok. Should I call out for today?"

"It couldn't hurt. I'll see you when you get here."

She giggled as she ended the call. Giggled. I tap the screen and call Chad. He answers on the first ring, "Hello favorite sister. How are you?"

"Good, I think. Glenda has a surprise for me and wants me to come over now. And call out of work. But she said you might be interested in the surprise too. If the surprise is what I think it is, how fast can you meet me at Glenda's?"

"You think she said yes?"

"It's the only thing I can think of for her to surprise both of us with."

"I'm at the property. I can be there in ten minutes."

"I'll see you there."

Ending the call, I call work as I am grabbing my purse and keys. I tell them a family emergency has come up and I can't come in. They are understanding and wish me well. I drop the phone in my lap as I back out of the driveway. I am just getting out of the car when Chad pulls up. He had to have been speeding. He is dressed in jeans and t-shirt, I ask, "Is today a work at the bar day or are you off?"

"Bar. They prefer the tight t-shirts. I wouldn't have them otherwise."

"I don't blame you. Let's get inside. I am dying to know what the surprise is."

The door opens as we draw near it, Glenda beaming out at us. "I thought you would never get here. Come back to the ritual room, both of you."

We follow Glenda back and she walks into the room, then immediately steps to the side. There is a woman standing in the middle of the room. She has a long, honey colored braid hanging down her back. She has an average size hourglass shape. Then she turns around and I see my face. An older version and some differences, but the resemblance is uncanny.

Chad says, "Holy shit, you look just like her."

The woman smiles. "She does look a lot like me."

Glenda is nearly bursting with joy, her hands clasped in front of her chest as she says, "Blaze, Chad, this is your grandmother, Serafina. Serafina, these are your grandchildren."

I don't know what to say, out of the million and one things I want to say, so I start with, "Hello. It's really nice to meet you."

She takes a step forward. "I am thrilled to meet you. I didn't know your mother had children. I'm so sorry we haven't met before now."

I look up at Chad and he looks at me. We both take a step toward her and he says, "We didn't know you existed. Mary thinks Pamela is her mother. Blaze was raised to believe she was her grandmother. I wasn't exactly part of the picture."

Serafina's jaw drops, and a single tear runs unchecked down her cheek. "I see that withdrawing for my own safety has had consequences I didn't foresee. It was my understanding that Mary planned to never have children. I suppose I shouldn't be surprised she was pressured into that as well. I saw the marriage announcement. Pamela made sure of it. What I don't understand is how you weren't part of things, Chad?"

He shrugs, "Well, she had me before she got married and I got left with our father. Blaze was born during the marriage."

Her brow crinkles as she puzzles over that and I explain, "It turns out that our mother can only have children with one particular man, a shifter named Erik. So we have the same father, regardless of what the birth certificate might say."

She laughs at that, loud and long. "Oh gods, Pamela must hate that so much! She is so big on everything appearing a certain way, only being with the right bloodlines, and your mother goes and has children with a shifter. It must make her head spin on her shoulders every time she thinks about it." She sobers and says, "I'm sorry you didn't get left with the father as well. I can only imagine how difficult she made your childhood since you were born with the audacity to be part shifter."

Shaking my head in agreement, I say, "It wasn't the most pleasant thing ever. I was relieved to learn about you. Would it be possible to spend some time with you? Maybe get to know you?"

Serafina smiles so wide I think her face might crack. "I would love that. But first, do you mind if I remove her tracking spell?"

"Her what? She has a tracking spell on me?"

Glenda asks, "Where? I haven't seen one."

Serafina says, "Just there, around her throat. My sister has always been good at hiding ugly things. And I have always been equally good at spotting them. May I remove it?"

"Yes, please do. No wonder she always seemed to be able to find me. Please, take it off." I walk forward, closing the distance between us.

Serafina puts her hands on either side of my neck and says, "This is probably going to hurt a lot. It's something she has always embedded into her spells."

I nod, "It's fine. I'll heal, and this will just be one more reason why she has to be stopped."

Serafina tips her head at what I said, but then

straightens and begins her spell. It burns and stings, as if I were burning up with a cold fire fueled by ghost pepper juice. Just as a scream of pain starts to bubble up from the depths of my soul, it stops. Opening eyes I didn't realize I had clenched shut, I see Serafina smiling at me. She says, "You are definitely a child of my line. May I hug you?"

"Yes, please, I would like that very much."

She wraps her arms around me and it feels exactly like I always imagined a grandmother hug should feel. Warm, comforting, and safe. I feel her lift and arm and wave Chad over. Suddenly, we are both a little crushed as he hugs us tightly.

When the hug ends, I feel like a little piece of the child I was is healed. Just a tiny piece, but it's a start. Serafina asks, "Would you like to have dinner with me? You are welcome to bring your significant others."

Chad snickers, and I glare at him. "Um, I have two. Will it be all right if they both come?"

Serafina exhales in relief. "Oh, it most certainly is. Now I don't need to worry about having any of my boyfriends hide when you are over. The more the merrier. Glenda, why don't you and Falina come over too?"

Glenda says, "We would love that."

I look at Chad, "Probably wouldn't be a terrible thing if we got Frankie to come along either, hmm?"

He blushes, "I didn't think anyone had noticed. Maybe better if you invite her. I haven't said anything to her."

I notice Serafina watching us, hands over her heart, pure joy on her face as the banter about whom to bring continues. Glenda steps up next to her and bumps shoulders with her. She says, "I am so happy for you. I know how much you missed your family." Serafina nods and I think Pamela has a lot to answer for and maybe, just maybe, we are the people to stop her. They say love can move mountains, maybe it can heal a broken family and stop an evil from taking over the world too.

Rhiannon Futch is a paranormal romance author and Chaos Coordinator, tarot deck collector, rescue dog mom, and craft enthusiast. She has been published since 2019 and is happily settled into writing vampire smut.

Record screech noise here Until the 2024 election she was happily settled into the one genre. Now she is also writing feminist horror novellas, blending her feminism with a dark nature and an immense well of feminine rage.

Wolfie, She-ra, and Daemon are her fully spoiled doggos who live for outdoor games and treat time. She is a night owl with a deep love of fall and winter and teaches yoga to authors but has never managed a headstand.

She is rarely found out in the world, preferring deep woods in the winter and cool writing spaces during the summer. Rhiannon lives in eastern North Carolina currently, with hopes of returning to the mountains of western North Carolina.

If you would like to see what books are next or sign up for her newsletter, visit rhiannonfutchauthor.com (You get a free book when you sign up!) You can also use the QR code (on the next page) to get to my website.

Also by Rhiannon Futch

The Daughter of the Moon series-

Selena Rose, Daughter of the Moon Book 1

Thorns of the Rose, Daughter of the Moon Book 2

Heart of the Rose, Daughter of the Moon Book 3

The Fate's Chronicles series

A Vampire's Fate

A Vampire's Treasure

A Vampire's Dream

A Vampire's Chase

A Vampire's Fight

Fated for Halloween - only available via email signup

The Belancore Witches of North Carolina series

Witchy Ever After

A Witchy New Year

My Witchy Valentine

Sin series

Sin on a Dark Knight

Sin on a Broken Heart

Sin on a Burning Heart

Sin on a Vengeful Heart

The Vampire Kings Series

Mercy of the Vampire King

Shame of the Vampire King

Pursuit of the Vampire King

Prey of the Vampire King

Reign of the Vampire King

Love and Vampires Series

Olivia's Fall

Olivia's Prison

Olivia's Flight

Olivia's Family

Warriors of the Old Gods series

A Dream of Blood

A Dream of Stone

A Dream of Ravens

A Dream of Bones

Her Violent Silence novella series

Wolf Goddess

Coyote Offerings

Old Wolf Woman

Witches Reclaimed series

Titles TBD